Spying on Jesus

Spying on Jesus

A Novella

RYAN AHLGRIM

RESOURCE *Publications* · Eugene, Oregon

SPYING ON JESUS
A Novella

Resource Publications
An Imprint of Wipf and Stock Publishers
199 W. 8th Ave., Suite 3
Eugene, OR 97401

www.wipfandstock.com

PAPERBACK ISBN: 979-8-3852-4368-6
HARDCOVER ISBN: 979-8-3852-4369-3
EBOOK ISBN: 979-8-3852-4370-9

VERSION NUMBER 031425

I

WHILE I WAS GROWING up, I thought my father was the smartest man in the world: literate, fluent in multiple languages, and an expert in the law and religious traditions. Townspeople greeted him with respect in the streets and deferred to his judgment in the synagogue. Because he was important, I was important.

My father was a scribe, as was his father, and his father's father, and his father's father's father; so it was my fate to be raised to become a scribe myself. Some sons rebel against their fathers and the occupation imposed upon them, but not me. I didn't choose to become a scribe, but if I could have, I would have. I loved learning how to read and write, and I thrived on studying Scripture and law, becoming a master of interpretation and application. My father taught me to be rigorous in my thinking, blending the wisdom of Torah with the logic of the Greeks. I became a formidable opponent as he and I debated the deepest meanings of each word, each letter in the sacred texts, as well as the arguments offered by the generations of scribes before us. One day in my eighteenth year he said, "Your argument was sounder than mine." It was my proudest moment.

My father died soon after I turned twenty-seven. Every comforting power over and above me evaporated, leaving me tottering on the tip of Mount Hermon, whipped by winds of nothing. Though the law remained, God had turned his face from me. Though married and blessed with a daughter, I was alone. Despite an absence of meaning or motivation, I took over my father's business: maintaining legal records for Galilee, financed by the government of Herod Antipas, the Tetrarch of Galilee and Perea.

Once a year I made the pleasant trek from my home in Sepphoris to Herod Antipas's palace in Tiberias—a city filled with grand architecture of recent construction, befitting the new capital. The hot springs, public baths, and serene views from the western slope of Lake Galilee made Tiberias a popular home for a multiethnic population of the privileged. Inside the bags strapped to my donkey I carried copies of the annual legal records of all of Galilee.

On my third trip to the capital, as I passed one layer of security after another—an inspection and bribe at the city gate, another inspection and interrogation at the palace gate, and yet another grilling and filling out of forms as I waited in the courtyard—I nearly lost my temper at all the mindless bureaucracy, paranoia, and petty corruption. I thought about how government is like marriage: you can't live with it, and you can't live without it. At its best, government provides military protection, trade, law courts, maybe a bit of justice, and enough social stability so that farmers keep us from starving to death. At its worst, it is an incomprehensible system of brutality and banditry. But at least it's organized. Without order, there's chaos. No matter how bad the government is, no government is worse—a condition resulting in perpetual violence and mass starvation.

I don't particularly like Herod Antipas's government, but it's the one the Romans allow us to have. There's no point working against it since the alternative is rebellion followed by an even more oppressive regime imposed by the Romans. So let's accept what is and do what good we can with what we have. Antipas's father, Herod the Great, ruled as a king over a much larger territory. He was far more adept at manipulating the Romans, managing the unruly population, and channeling money into grand construction projects and needed infrastructure. He was ruthless, hated by many, but he left an impressive visible legacy. I wish Antipas possessed his father's political skills, if not his viciousness.

As I began unpacking my records on a large wooden table in a room bristling with scrolls, an attendant entered. "Come with me. Theodorus wants to see you."

Theodorus? My father had introduced me to him a few years before, afterwards whispering in my ear, "He's Herod's spy chief." Why would Theodorus want to see me? Though I tried to hide it, panic raced through my veins. Had someone accused me of fiddling with the books? Was I just moments away from being hauled off to prison to be tortured? When interacting with the levers of power, life is always balanced on the edge of a dagger.

I could feel my ears burning and turning red as I followed the attendant down a long hall, up two flights of stairs, and around a corner to a closed door. The attendant knocked. "Come in," came a voice from within. The attendant opened the door and announced me.

"Caleb the scribe, sir."

A man twice my age with rheumy eyes and a scowling face sat at a small desk facing me. "Sit down," he said with a husky voice, motioning toward a chair facing him. I sat.

"Caleb, I knew your father. Do you remember meeting me on one of his trips here to the palace?"

"Yes, we met in the courtyard," I replied softly.

"And now you do what he used to do—going around to all the villages of Galilee on legal business."

"Yes."

"So you meet a lot of people and hear a lot of things."

My anxiety lessened. Instead of him making an accusation against me, it sounded like he wanted me to confirm an accusation against someone else.

"Yes, I know all the village elders; I hear a lot of gossip."

"Good. I have a job for you."

Fear drained out of my body. *I won't die today*, I thought to myself. A job, any job, was better than the prospect of defending myself against anonymous accusations, as I well knew from a past painful experience.

"What do you want me to do?"

He pressed his fingertips together. "I hear there's a trouble-maker stirring up the peasants around Capernaum. According to my sources, he's a follower of the Baptizer. Now that the Baptizer is in prison, I'm wondering if this new demagogue may be taking up the reins of the Baptizer's protest movement. I need to know how dangerous he is. What exactly is he saying and doing? How many people are listening to him? Does he have followers? Is he a credible threat to Herod's popularity or to the government's stability? Is he saying anything treasonous? Are there legal grounds for arresting him? That's what I want you to find out. It should be easy. He's nearby, so track him down, keep your ears and eyes open, and bring a report back to me."

I glanced away from his steady stare. Though I had no sympathy for bandits, terrorists, rioters, and those who egged them on with religious fanaticism, I did not want to be the one who caused the torture and execution of another.

"Most excellent Theodorus, I would be honored to help you at the beginning of next week, after I have finished archiving the annual records. Perhaps someone else is more immediately available?"

"You can do the archiving later. I need this information now while he's still in the area. You'll be paid a hundred denarii if you come back here before the end of the week with a complete report."

This was not a request. I did not dare to inquire what would happen if I did not carry out this assignment, but the money mollified me.

"What's his name?"

"Jesus of Nazareth."

"Nazareth?" I asked with surprise, wondering if I may have met the man. I knew that village. A tiny place just a few miles from Sepphoris.

"Have you ever heard of him?"

"No."

"That's a good sign. Maybe he's not as popular as I've heard. The last thing we need is another Baptizer criticizing the government and convincing people it's the end of the world."

I nodded.

Theodorus folded his hands. "That's all. You may leave."

II

"You who are suffering in poverty are lucky because God's empire belongs to you! But you who are rich are out of luck!"

The words startled me.

"You who are starving are lucky because you'll be fed with all that you need! But you who are full are out of luck—you'll be starving!"

Wait a minute, I thought to myself.

"You who are crying out in pain are lucky because you'll soon be laughing! But you who are laughing are out of luck—you'll be crying!"

My temper was rising.

The speaker's rough clothing, weathered face, and calloused hands marked him as a laborer. How strange that this uneducated country rube, barely out of his twenties, would think he could turn the world topsy-turvy simply by saying so. And yet his fervor was doing just that, casting a spell of excitement over the eager crowd. The tenant farmers, day laborers, fishermen, and the homeless, who were gathered in the marketplace of Capernaum overlooking the north shore of Lake Galilee, shouted a frenzied cheer. Along the fringes of the crowd and in the stalls stood a few landowners and merchants who shrank back in dismay, partly afraid the crowd might attack them, but also wondering if the Almighty was about to reach down out of the clouds to sweep away the rich and powerful.

The speaker continued to stoke the resentments of the poor, filling their minds with fantasies. Theodorus was right to be concerned about this man. He might indeed be sowing sedition and preparing to lead a revolt against the government. After further pronouncements of impending judgment, the speaker left the marketplace. Half the crowd surged after him.

I knew I was only supposed to observe, record, and report, but my indignation welled up in me. I could not stand the thought of this ignorant fanatic going unchallenged, poisoning these simple minds and creating trouble. I pushed my way through the crowd and raised my voice.

"Teacher! So you're in favor of class warfare?"

The speaker stopped, turned around, and looked me up and down, sizing me up: a scribe, not wealthy but not poor, secure in a government job. I expected some sort of dismissive response, or perhaps a suggestion that someone in the crowd should box my ears. Instead, he answered me calmly.

"It is the rich who are engaged in warfare. They are indifferent to human need while their greediness demands more wealth for themselves. God wills all people to have enough, so God's empire will abolish this injustice. Even now it is dawning, sending its rays throughout the world."

I wasn't sure he had answered my question. I pressed him again. "Is God going to shut out those who worked hard for their wealth? Isn't wealth a gift from God?"

He pounced: "You can't serve two masters! They will inevitably make opposite demands. You can't serve God and money."

That was ludicrous. "Didn't God bless Abraham with many flocks?"

After staring at me for several seconds, he turned to address the crowd.

"There once was a rich man. He wore the purple of the aristocracy; he dined on imported delicacies; he led a life of carefree excess."

I could see people in the crowd shaking their heads in disgust.

"At the front gate of his mansion sat a homeless man, sick and covered in sores. He begged for food and small coins from those who walked by, and he rummaged through the rich man's garbage to survive."

I heard grunts. Everyone saw this scenario every day.

"The poor man died, and God's angels took his soul to paradise where he was welcomed by Abraham. The rich man also died, and his soul descended into the Pit, where he was tormented."

Someone behind me muttered, "Serves him right."

"The rich man looked up and saw the poor man in paradise with Abraham. He cried out, 'Abraham, have mercy on me! Send that poor man to bring me a cup of cool water!' But Abraham replied, 'Son, during your lifetime you had everything you needed and a lot more besides. This poor man, who lived at your gate, had nothing but misery. Now he's comforted and you are in distress. Isn't that fair? Did you ever do anything to change the injustice? But it's too late now; the gulf between us can't be crossed.'"

I could see many nods as the crowd yearned for an afterlife that worked this way.

"The rich man said, 'Then I beg you to send that poor man back to my five brothers to warn them that they have to change before it's too late.' Abraham replied, 'They already have the laws of Moses and the warnings of the prophets. They should listen to them!'"

The speaker's last words rang in the air in judgment. He then turned away from me, walked a few steps down a narrow street, and into a house.

That was my first encounter with Jesus of Nazareth.

III

Caleb the scribe to Theodorus:

May God bless you and the soul of Herod Antipas, our beloved Tetrarch.

I found Jesus of Nazareth preaching in Capernaum to a crowd of perhaps a hundred people, mostly peasants. He is attacking the wealthy for accumulating wealth, claiming God will punish them and give rewards instead to the poor. He claims "God's empire" is about to be established. I did not see any armed followers or hear any plans for rebellion. Nevertheless, he is stirring up discontent against the current system. He has a forceful, charismatic personality and a flair for imagery in his speaking.

At this point I am not sure what level of threat he may pose or what legal actions could be taken against him. I need a little more time. I request you give me several more days to investigate before I return to you with a full report.

God's peace be with you and our Tetrarch.

Two days later a messenger arrived at my lodgings in Capernaum with Theodorus's response.

Theodorus to Caleb the scribe:

Our God is great, and our Tetrarch is beneficent. Blessings in God's name.

Your report aroused concern in Herod's court. You are hereby temporarily relieved of your scribal duties and ordered by the Tetrarch to continue monitoring Jesus of Nazareth on an ongoing basis until you are recalled. Send regular reports to me through government messengers. We want to know where he is at all times, what he is saying and doing, his plans, as well as receive updated threat assessments and your analysis of his legal vulnerabilities.

With fervent prayers for your success.

When I read this, I kicked a mat across the room. I'm a scribe, not a spy. I cursed myself for sending Theodorus a request to investigate for a few more days; now I was stuck in this investigation with no end in sight. Part of me wondered how I was supposed to do this new assignment. How was I to monitor Jesus's movements without being noticed and arousing suspicion? More distressing was the thought of someone else doing my scribal work in my absence. Would they mess up my records?

After a half hour of fretting and pacing the room, my steps slowed. I stopped and looked up at the thatched ceiling. The idea of spying on this fanatic wasn't all bad. I didn't know how I would do it, but I started imagining possibilities. My talent for research, detail, and debate might be a good fit for this task. Maybe Theodorus had seen this potential in me all along. This assignment would mean having to skip visits home to see my wife and young daughter—at least for now. I could accept that. I felt important.

IV

"Watch out for greed! It's easier for a camel to squeeze through the eye of a needle than for a rich man to get into God's empire!"

Jesus was still in Capernaum slamming the rich. To my surprise, the crowds had gotten larger, so much so that he had moved out of the marketplace and was now on the open beach where two or three hundred people were crowding around him. To make himself heard, he got into a boat and had a fisherman row him out a short distance so that his voice would be amplified by the water.

"A farmer who owned extensive lands had bumper crops last year. He had so much extra grain he couldn't fit it into his barns. What do you think he did? Did he share his excess crops with his neighbors who were hungry? Did he share with those who, because of accidents and disease, could no longer work? No. He decided instead to pull down his existing barns and build even bigger ones so he could save more for himself. He thought to himself, 'I now have enough food stored up to take care of myself for the rest of my life. I don't have to work anymore. I'll just relax and throw parties with my friends from now on.' But that same night God came to him and said, 'You're a fool! I have come to take your life. How are all your possessions and wealth going to help you now?'"

He told another story about a rich merchant who went on a lengthy business trip, leaving various managers in charge of his wealth while he was gone. When he returned, he gave extravagant bonuses to those managers who most increased his wealth, and he fired the one manager who refused, on moral grounds, to lend out money at high interest to make more money. He concluded by saying, "Those who have more, get more, while those who have less, the little they have gets taken away." It was an indictment of our economic system. In his eyes, using wealth to get more wealth while others descend into greater poverty and indebtedness was an affront to God, and God was coming in judgment to change it all and punish the greedy.

The crowd ate it up. They cheered. They chanted. The whole message was hopelessly naïve.

Jesus motioned to the fisherman who then rowed him to shore. Stepping out of the boat onto the dark gray rocks of the beach, he made his way through the crowd, back into town, and into a house. The crowd surrounded the house, filling the court-yard for hours, but he didn't come out. Shortly before sunset, because it was Friday, the massive crowd finally dissipated and went to their homes for the Sabbath. I went back to the inn where I was staying and fought a losing battle against the lice.

The next morning I got up early and went outside. Being the Sabbath, the streets were empty and quiet. No fishermen got up early to fish. No farmers sold their produce. No wagons rattled on the cobblestones. But gradually doors began to open and I saw streams of people heading for the synagogue, including Jesus followed by several men. I fell into step behind them.

When we arrived at the synagogue, it was nearly full. Men sat shoulder to shoulder on the ascending steps wrapped around the back and side walls. I managed to squeeze myself into a spot high up along the back wall, while Jesus and his companions were offered space on the bottom step near the front. Before long, the room was at capacity, and many were forced to stand in the back, in the doorway, or outside. The synagogue leader, a man with a long, gray-tinged beard and reedy voice, led the assembly in the Sabbath prayers and songs. After the songs, he asked Jesus to offer the Scripture reading and commentary.

Jesus stood, walked to the Scripture box, took out a scroll, unrolled it on a small table, and began to read in a resonant, passionate voice: "The spirit of the Lord has fallen on me, because the Lord has anointed me. He has sent me to bring good news to the oppressed, to bind up the wounds of those with a broken spirit, to proclaim freedom for captives, release for prisoners, and to announce that this is the year of the Lord's liberation!"

He then rolled up the scroll of Isaiah the prophet and placed it back in the box. He walked to his seat, sat down, and looked at everyone with a stare that built up tension.

"Today," he boomed, "this Scripture has been fulfilled in your presence!"

His declaration was so arrogant, the walls of the synagogue should have collapsed. He was claiming to be God's special agent for carrying out Isaiah's vision. It was breathtaking if you believed it, and outrageous if you did not. No dry sermon or pious platitudes this morning!

As if on cue, a scrawny man with wild eyes, who was standing at the door, began howling like a wounded dog and then shouted, "Don't destroy us, Jesus of Nazareth! Don't destroy us! The light of God is burning!"

The man raced forward, screaming, tearing at his hair. Some men called out his name and tackled him. They held him on the floor as he kicked and bit at those trying to restrain him. I felt as if I was sitting in a theater watching a comical play tumbling with mad actors. I didn't know who was more unhinged—Jesus of Nazareth or this poor fellow suffering from insanity.

Then Jesus stood up, calmly walked over to the thrashing man, put his hands on his head, whispered something in his ear, and then said in a roaring voice, "Unclean spirit, come out of this man. He is free!"

The man let out one more long howl that gradually drifted away. His body relaxed, and the men on top of him were able to let go of their grip. The man laid there, panting, and then sighed. A look of exhaustion transitioned into peacefulness.

What had I just witnessed? A charade? An exorcism? The steadying voice of authority? Any seemed possible. The assembly, though, had few doubts: people started jabbering about God's power unleashed in the world and the overthrow of Satan's reign.

Jesus swiftly left the synagogue. Since it was the Sabbath, everyone went straight home, and I wandered back to my room, contemplating what I had just witnessed and how to report it.

That evening, as soon as the sun dipped below the horizon, I saw massive crowds heading to the house where Jesus was staying. But this time there was an inordinately large number of ill people among them, all begging for God's healing power. I couldn't get any closer than a stone's throw, but from where I stood in the street, I could see Jesus at the doorway of the house putting his hands on one person after another, all evening long. Some people walked away shouting for joy in evident relief. Surely this was a kind of mass hysteria. People were so desperate for healing and hope, they convinced themselves that God's power had touched them.

> Caleb the scribe to Theodorus:
>
> The blessing of our almighty God be with Herod Antipas to rule us with wisdom and justice.
>
> Jesus of Nazareth continues to be active in Capernaum, and, unfortunately, his popularity is expanding. Not only are his pronouncements against the wealthy hitting a nerve among the peasants, but now he has become known as a healer and exorcist, attracting additional crowds through magic or subterfuge. Most alarming, he is claiming to be the prophet spoken of by Isaiah—the one who announces the coming of God's liberation for the oppressed. This is stoking revolutionary hopes among the peasants. Can Jesus keep this fantasy going, or will disillusionment soon return people to reason? Perhaps there is a chance this movement will fizzle out on its own. I'll keep watching.
>
> God's mercy be with the Tetrarch.

V

THE NEXT DAY, TO my astonishment, Jesus was gone from Capernaum. No one seemed to know where he had gone, so he must have left before dawn. I packed my bag and set off on foot to the nearest villages to see if I could find him. In the late afternoon I heard from a trader that he was in Bethsaida, a large fishing town just over the border in the tetrarchy of Philip. When I got there the town was buzzing with excitement, and I found Jesus once again addressing a large crowd on the shore of the lake. Wrapping up his message, he shifted to a recruiting drive:

"Sell your possessions and give the money to those in the most need. Then follow me and I'll teach you to fish for humanity!"

A few people clamored to follow him, offering to quit their jobs and leave their homes at that very moment. One man, though, said, "Let me bury my father first, and then I'll follow you."

Jesus immediately responded, "Let the dead bury the dead. Follow me now."

I was stunned by Jesus's callousness toward this man's grief and his disrespect for the man's obligation to honor his father. Seeing the dismay in the man's face, and perhaps in a lot of other faces as well, Jesus turned to the crowd and doubled down on his demand: "Unless you hate your father and mother, brothers and sisters, wife and children, and even your own life, you cannot be my disciple."

Hyperbole? I assumed so, but it was still remarkable arrogance to put loyalty to himself above loyalty to one's family.

One young man, now uncertain and confused, asked, "May I say goodbye to my family?"

"No one who puts his hand to the plow and looks back is fit for God's empire," Jesus replied.

How could the crowd not see that Jesus was creating a personality cult demanding complete control over his followers' lives? And yet, he whipped up world-ending fervor with such compelling images that several men—mostly fishermen who weren't tied to the land—agreed on the spot to become his itinerant disciples.

That's when I realized I had a golden opportunity before me. Why not offer to follow him myself? Rather than being a bystander on the fringes, I could have direct access to Jesus and keep tabs on him at all times. This could be the ultimate intelligence coup.

On the other hand, what would happen if Jesus were to find out I was spying on him for Herod's government? What would he do to me? And if Herod's police decided to arrest Jesus, would I be in danger of getting caught up in the dragnet? Would I be able to get word to Theodorus to release me before I was tortured? The risks were real. I am not a courageous man when it comes to possible pain. But the potential rewards appeared to outweigh the risks.

But would Jesus accept me as a disciple? I was obviously in a different class than these peasants. Would Jesus really want someone like me—an educated government employee? Wouldn't I be under constant suspicion? After all, I had challenged him in my first encounter with him. But what was the worst that could happen? He could say no. If he did, I could still hang around the edges of his movement and keep him under surveillance. I decided I needed to act quickly while the recruitment door was still open.

"Teacher!" I shouted, pushing myself forward. "I'm ready to go with you wherever you go."

Jesus, looking at my soft features and linen clothing, shook his head. "Foxes have holes and birds have nests, but I will have no comfortable places to lay my head."

I decided to use my scriptural knowledge to impress him. "Where you go, I'll go. Where you lodge, I'll lodge. Your people will be my people, and your God, my God."

I smiled but he did not smile back at me. Instead he replied, "You forgot the most important part: 'Where you die, I will die—there will I be buried.' Is that the commitment you're making?"

That wiped the smile off my face. I could feel little tremors in my arms, hands, and jaw which I tried to control. What a stupid idea it was to ask to join this man, but I put my fears aside and quietly completed Ruth's words of commitment to Naomi:

"May the Lord do thus and more to me if even death parts me from you."

He nodded solemnly. "Come with me."

VI

Caleb the scribe to Theodorus:

God be thanked for his guidance and mercy.

I have successfully infiltrated Jesus's circle of followers by becoming one of his itinerant disciples. I will now
be able to collect significantly more detailed information
about Jesus's plans and activities. However, my reports
may be sporadic since it may be difficult for me to send
these reports through the network of government messengers without being detected.

The number of itinerant disciples following Jesus is
currently nineteen. Within this group is an inner circle
called "the Twelve." They are with Jesus at all meals and
lodging. Jesus selected them to represent the twelve
tribes of Israel, the first step in reconstituting the nation
of Israel. This in itself suggests that he plans to replace
the governments of Herod, Philip, and Pontius Pilate.

Within the Twelve is a bodyguard of three burly men
who are with him constantly. The most prominent is a
massive man named Simon Bar-Jonah, but he is usually
known by a nickname given to him by Jesus: Rock. He
has a brother, Andrew, but he's not sufficiently imposing
and aggressive to be part of the bodyguard. Another set
of brothers completes the bodyguard: James and John
Bar-Zebedee. These two fellows act like thugs, ready to
break the arms of anyone who looks at Jesus the wrong
way. They well deserve their nicknames: Sons of Thunder.

The remaining seven of us who are not within the
Twelve usually fend for ourselves. The entire group of

twenty is too large for any but the most affluent homes to host us all, so we seven often do our own begging to get whatever food and lodging we can.

Shockingly, our itinerant band is currently being accompanied by a group of prosperous women who provide funds to assist us with food and lodging when we can't find a host. One of the women is Mary of Magdala. She became a follower when Jesus cast seven demons out of her. (Perhaps she still has one or two.) Most disturbing is the presence of a woman named Joanna whom I immediately recognized as the wife of Herod's steward, Chuza. It would be quite embarrassing for Herod's government if it became known that Chuza's wife is traveling with Jesus and providing funds! Thankfully, she is keeping a low profile and hides her identity from the crowds and our hosts. As it is, the presence of this group of women is a scandal, though I should add that Jesus insists on marital fidelity; he condemns any thoughts of lust by men for married women.

Regarding Jesus's teachings, yesterday I heard him tell someone, "I did not come to bring peace, but a sword. I've come to set a man against his father, a daughter against her mother, a daughter-in-law against her mother-in-law. Your enemies will be members of your own household." Jesus is actively splitting families by insisting on absolute loyalty to himself and his message. By doing so, he is tearing down the supportive fabric of society, creating hostility, and sowing the seeds of violence. He is a dangerous fanatic.

We are currently in Gennesaret. I don't know how long we will be here.

Based on the increased risks I am incurring, and the unknown length of time I will be serving you in this capacity, I humbly request that my compensation be reconsidered. Might it be possible for half of the promised one hundred denarii to be sent now to my wife in Sepphoris for her support, and might an additional bonus be paid to my account for each week that I am in your special employment, beginning now?

With God's aid, we will prevail.

VII

Now that I was one of Jesus's itinerant followers, with him constantly, I found myself drowning in stories. If Jesus wasn't telling a perturbing parable, he was using bizarre analogies and metaphors. Sometimes it was clear what he meant, but at other times his illustrations were head-scratching or open to diverse interpretations. For instance, consider this story:

"Listen! A farmer was casting his seed in the field. Some seeds landed on the path. It didn't take root; instead, the birds quickly ate it. Some seed landed among rocks. The thin soil allowed it to take root, but because it had no depth, the hot sun scorched the young plants and they withered away. Some seeds landed in the weeds. It took root but was eventually choked out by the weeds. But some seeds landed on good soil. It grew and produced a harvest yielding sometimes thirty, or sixty, or even a hundred times what had been sown."

What is this story about? The difficulties of being a farmer? A metaphor about the dangers of following Jesus? Or is Jesus saying something about God's empire? More broadly, is this story meant to be a warning or an encouragement? Is it telling us to beware, or is it telling us not to give up in the face of many failures? Is it a promise of a good result if we persist? Or is it telling us that God persists, so have hope?

Consider this other story he told a woman who hosted us for supper:

"In one town there was a judge who didn't care about God's will or people's welfare. A poor widow came to his court demanding justice. She kept insisting, 'My landlord is cheating me!' The judge tried ignoring her, dismissing her again and again, but she kept coming back to court. Finally, he said to himself, 'Even though I don't care about God's will or people's welfare, because she keeps bugging me, I'll give her justice. I'm tired of her pummeling me!'"

This one stumped me. I wanted to ask Rock what the story meant since Rock was Jesus's right-hand man, but Rock was so physically imposing and intimidating, and seemed to have such a high degree of antipathy towards me, that I instead sought out one of the other members of the Twelve, a stonemason named Thaddaeus.

"It's obviously about prayer," he smirked, enjoying his peasant superiority over my scriptural education. "Like the widow, we should keep pleading for what is right until God gives it to us."

This didn't make sense to me. I decided to show him who was the ignorant one.

"Prayer? You've got to be kidding me! Do you think prayer is about wearing down God with our complaints until God, wearied of us, finally gives in? That would mean the judge in this story is supposed to represent God. But how can he represent God when the judge himself says he doesn't care about God's will or people's welfare?"

Thaddaeus's face turned red and his nostrils flared. "You think you're so smart, don't you? The point is that if a wicked judge will do what's right if we persist, how much more will God give us justice if we persist!"

That was a wiser response than I was expecting, but I wasn't about to tell Thaddaeus that. Besides, I wasn't convinced.

"You're still making the mistake of thinking prayer is about wearing down God. What if this story isn't about prayer?"

Thaddaeus tilted his head back and forth in a teasing way as he asked, "Then what do you think the story is about, know-it-all?"

I put my knuckles on my hips as I thought for a moment.

"What if," I started hesitantly, "what if it's the widow—not the judge—who is supposed to be like God? What if the judge represents all the forces of injustice and indifference in the world?

Maybe the story is about how God keeps chiseling away, no matter how hopeless it seems, until justice emerges from a massive boulder." I smiled triumphantly.

Thaddaeus let out an exasperated breath and stomped away. I enjoyed beating him in this argument, but to be honest, I wasn't sure about my interpretation of the story. Can God possibly be compared to a poor widow? Is God so powerless?

The next day Jesus told a story that was even more confusing and—frankly—offensive:

"God's empire is like a landowner who went out at dawn to the marketplace to hire laborers to work in his vineyard. He agreed to pay them a denarius. At nine o'clock he went back to the marketplace to hire some more laborers, promising to pay them 'what is right.' At noon he hired some more, and at three o'clock still more. At five o'clock he went back to the marketplace and found a few laborers standing around. 'Why aren't you working?' he asked them. 'No one will hire us,' they answered. He told them to go to his vineyard as well. At six o'clock he told the manager to call in all the laborers and pay them, beginning with those who worked the shortest amount of time. Those who worked one hour received a denarius, as did those who worked part of the day. Those at the end of the line, who had worked all day, assumed they'd be paid more. Instead, they also received a denarius. They complained about how unfair it was that they had worked the entire day in the scorching heat and yet received the same pay as those who had worked only one hour. The landowner responded, 'Friend, I haven't wronged you. I've paid you exactly what we agreed to. It's up to me if I want to give these others the same pay. Are you going to give me the evil eye because I'm good?'"

How is this like God's empire? I wanted to ask Jesus or one of the Twelve, but the Twelve were all giving me the cold shoulder, and, like a shield, kept blocking my access to Jesus. So I had to just mull over the story on my own.

The landowner claims to be good, and yet he pays everyone the same no matter how hard and long they've worked. I would have complained too! Those laborers who worked one hour did not deserve to get a full denarius. Not only had they put in very little labor, they also probably weren't competent workers to begin with—which would explain why they were still unhired in the marketplace at five o'clock. It's a basic tenet of fairness that we should get paid according to how good our work is and how long we've been doing it. I could not see how Jesus, who was always preaching about justice, could compare God's empire to something so blatantly unfair.

One evening I managed to sneak past the vigilance of the Twelve and asked Jesus to tell me the meaning of these stories. He raised his eyebrow and said, "Do you want me to chew your bread for you?"

I ask him to explain his metaphors, and all I get is another metaphor.

VIII

I HAD LITTLE IN common with these rural rustics who were blindly following Jesus, and they knew it. Not only did they resent my education and distrust me, they were also jealous if I managed to snatch a brief conversation with Jesus. They considered themselves the specially chosen and so they wanted Jesus all to themselves. Nevertheless, after a few weeks they began to loosen up a little around me, and I was surprised to find myself experiencing a sense of group solidarity with them.

I suppose it was due to sharing all those meals, and sleeping together in barns, and depending on each other for our day-to-day survival. It was more difficult for me than for them. Constant traveling on foot was nothing new to me, but my diet was considerably coarser and smaller than what I was used to. Nor did I enjoy the lack of privacy every night and the frequent noise of running rodents about my head while I tried to sleep. Worst of all was the indignity of begging for food and lodging day after day in every town we came to. But these shared hardships gradually created camaraderie among us. Each of us possessed habits that irked the others, but after a while some of those habits became sources of friendly amusement, even fondness.

I was surprised to discover that Bartholomew, one of the Twelve, with the bushiest beard and biggest belly, possessed a rare wit that kept us laughing even in the face of disappointments. Philip, the youngest among the Twelve, with a cheerful and innocent nature, expressed surprising insights now and then.

One day, while Philip and I were pulling water out of a well and filling skins, I asked him why he had joined Jesus.

"Because the world is messed up and I think this guy knows how to change it."

"How can begging in the streets change anything?"

"How can it not?"

"What do you mean?"

"It's only when we give up everything and give up doing the things we've always done before that we provoke change."

I hadn't thought of it that way before. Risking offense, I asked, "But isn't Jesus acting like a dictator by demanding total loyalty?"

Philip filled another skin while I held the mouth open. He then looked at me and thoughtfully replied, "A dictator serves himself. Have you seen any selfishness in Jesus at all?"

I had to admit I had not. Nevertheless, Jesus kept saying and doing things that alarmed me. The Twelve had fallen under his spell, but no matter how much I was starting to feel like a part of the group, I was determined to keep a certain emotional distance and think for myself.

Later that afternoon, while Jesus was speaking to a family struggling to pay rent to their landlord, he told them, "Don't worry about survival."

This was a refrain I had heard him say repeatedly. He would tell farmers after locusts ate their crops, "Don't worry about food." He'd tell people whose wells had run dry, "Don't worry about water." He'd tell naked beggars, "Don't worry about clothes." I couldn't understand why these peasants didn't tar and feather him or at least laugh him out of town for saying such nonsense. But after hearing him say this to a family desperate for something besides platitudes, I couldn't hold back any longer. As soon as we were alone, I said to him, "Jesus, how can you tell these people not to worry? Their lives are on the line! You're dismissing their misery and distress."

Jesus could hear the distress in my voice, and could probably see the tightness in my jaw. Calmly he asked, "Will worry help them?"

I didn't answer, so he went on. "Will worrying about bread make it appear? Will worrying about water create a spring? Will worrying about survival add an inch to their lives?"

"But they have good reason to worry!" I insisted.

"Worry is useless," he responded. "It is worse than useless—it degrades us. It tempts us to become selfish and closed-fisted. It drives us to make life about ourselves. When we worry, we are not trusting in God; we are not even believing in God."

I wanted to say, "That's ridiculous," but settled for, "I don't see that."

"Look at the birds in the sky," he suggested as a flock of starlings turned and circled overhead. "They don't plant or harvest or store up food in barns, yet God feeds them. Doesn't God value us more than the birds? Or look at the wildflowers growing in that field. Even Solomon was never clothed as beautifully as those flowers. If God gives flowers such extravagant glory—though today they bloom and tomorrow they are burned as fuel—won't God clothe us with what we need?"

"No," I blurted. I decided it was time for some hard truths. "Birds die of starvation, and so do we. Flowers die from the cold, and so do we. God doesn't stop terrible things from happening to people no matter how much they trust in God."

"True," sighed Jesus. "The devil brings calamity to as many as he can. He wants us to give up on goodness and God. He wants us to become evil and selfish like himself. But God is the ruler of the universe, not the devil. The birds and flowers show us God's abundant delight in life. Despite all the diseases and droughts and acts of evil, God's love for his good creation continues. It cannot be stopped. We are not like the Gentiles who believe in gods who are indifferent and immoral. We belong to a God whose love is constant, never deserting us, no matter what evil may befall us. That's why our survival is not the purpose of life."

"Then what is life's purpose?"

"To strive for what is right and good. We do not live to survive. We live for God's empire."

I shook my head. "So you're telling these poor peasants with empty plates that they should live for God's empire instead of trying to survive?"

Jesus's eyes bored into me. "God's empire *is* their survival. What do you think God's empire is?"

Despite chewing on the bread of his stories for a long time, their point continued to elude me.

"I don't know."

"You've been with me these many weeks and still you don't know?"

I shook my head in embarrassment.

"It's sharing. We share all we have with one another so that everyone has enough. It's doing for others what we would want them to do for us. It's loving everyone the same way we love ourselves. It's renouncing hate and grudges so we can be reconciled to one another. If we do this, we will do far more than survive. We will be the children of God and God's peace will rule the earth."

Now I was really confused. "But I heard you say that you've come to bring a sword to the earth, not peace."

"Loving our neighbors as we love ourselves is so contrary to how the world lives, many will oppose it, especially those who have more and do not want to share, and those with power who do not want to serve, and those who have been hurt who want to hit back. God is shaking the greedy and vengeful foundations of this world! Some will join God's empire, and some will not. It is their own choice to be left out."

I began to wonder if I had misinterpreted some of his teachings.

"Caleb, look at what we are doing. We are going from town to town as beggars with nothing but the Spirit of God. We preach the good news that God's empire is invading and pushing back Satan's empire. Those who are in despair, we are filling with hope. Those who are ill, we are giving relief. In return, we rely on their generosity—whatever little they may have—to provide us with a bed for the night and a crust of bread for our stomachs. By doing this we are together practicing what it means to trust in God and walk in love. This is the dawning of God's empire."

For a second I glimpsed the glory of what he was saying and I almost believed it, but he was too naïve. Human nature does not change, and our political and economic systems do not change. If they are overthrown, the usurpers simply become a mirror of those they overthrew; the good guys and bad guys change places, and new oppressions replace the old oppressions.

Jesus could see the wheels turning in my head, suspecting my doubts. "Caleb," he announced, "I'm giving you a new name. From now on I'm calling you 'Watcher.' You stand aside and you watch."

The nickname unsettled me. Did he know I was a spy?

IX

AFTER SPENDING SEVERAL DAYS in Gennesaret and then Chorazin, we crossed the border into the tetrarchy of Philip. At the border, on the road running alongside Lake Galilee, was a toll booth. Every traveler had to pay a toll to enter the territory of Philip the Tetrarch. Rock and the Sons of Thunder were arguing with the toll collector, accusing him of extortion because he had changed the toll rate from the day before. Jesus raised his hand to quiet his bodyguards and told one of the Twelve who held the common purse to pay the toll for our group.

Then Jesus looked at the toll collector and said, "I saw you yesterday listening to me." The man nodded. Jesus then announced, "I'm having dinner with you tonight. I want you to follow me."

That was the way Jesus spoke to people: directly, confidently, with total ease. His aura of authority was unlike anything I had ever experienced before. I'd met plenty of people who get their way through physical threats or fast talking, intimidation or credentials, pomposity or tearful hard-luck stories; and I'd met people who get their way through schmoozing and winning smiles and asking about your kids; but Jesus wasn't like any of them. He convinced others through an effortless of-course-ness. This wasn't just charisma—this was godlike. In his presence I felt as if I was standing in a protective sphere of spiritual power—as ridiculous as that sounds.

The toll collector wavered.

Jesus asked him, "What's your name?" The young man said his name was Levi, son of Alpheus. Jesus smiled, beckoned with his hand, and said, "Levi, son of Alpheus, follow me."

Jesus then walked away. The toll collector hesitated a moment, grabbed his money bag, and then left the booth. By this point in my time with Jesus, I was not surprised.

We had dinner that evening at Levi's house. He turned it into a party for the impious, inviting all his toll collector colleagues and other men whose occupations involved ignoring religious regulations and social mores. It was a boisterous supper. Through his occupation, Levi had squeezed a lot of money out of his fellow citizens, so he had plenty of food and wine to share, and Jesus showed no scruples in enjoying the horn of plenty.

I found myself unable to join the revelry of the evening. Despite the grumbling of my empty stomach, participating in this meal was ethically offensive and inconsistent with what Jesus had been teaching. How could I eat and drink that which came through the cheating of tax collectors? I have no objection to governments collecting fair and moderate taxes in order to function properly. My own salary as a scribe comes through taxation. But I can't abide tax collectors who, after getting their jobs through a bidding process, set the tax rate at whatever they think the market can bear and then reap massive profits. How could I laugh and share food with men who so disrespected Moses's laws? Why was Jesus, a man who posed as a prophet, associating with them so freely and enjoyably?

"What's the matter, Watcher?" Jesus saw that my plate and cup remained untouched.

"I'm not hungry tonight," I lied. "Queasy stomach."

Jesus turned to the other diners. "If a shepherd has a hundred sheep and one of them wanders off, what does the shepherd do? Does he stay with the ninety-nine and accept the loss of the one, or does he leave the flock on the hillside and look for that one that wandered off?" Answering his own question, he said, "If he finds it, he puts it across his shoulders and carries it back, feeling more joy for that one sheep that was found than for the ninety-nine that never strayed."

And then came the pivot.

"Levi, God wants to find you. Stop defrauding travelers, make restitution, and give your wealth to the poor. From now on let nothing but honest words flow from your mouth."

Everyone reclining around the table froze in place.

"Do this," Jesus concluded, "and the angels will rejoice in heaven!"

His words made the hairs on my neck stand up. Would Levi become enraged that he was being confronted in his own home, in front of his friends? Or had Jesus paved a path of respect by requesting Levi's hospitality and accepting bread from his table, ignoring questions of whether the food was unclean or ill-gotten?

Levi melted. The next day he left his house and business behind, joining us on the road.

As we walked along, Jesus sidled up to me and said softly, "It's the ones who are sick who need a doctor, not the ones who are well. We're here to heal the sick, and that means sitting at their tables and accepting their food."

Caleb the scribe to Theodorus:

I remember you and our sovereign every day in my prayers.

I'm sorry to report that Jesus of Nazareth's influence continues to increase. I am shocked by the coalition of followers he has managed to pull together. In addition to tenant farmers, craftsmen, and fishermen, he has also enlisted the active support of a significant number of tax collectors! I still can't quite understand how he pulls this off. One tax collector has joined him as an itinerant disciple. This motley group of followers, who would otherwise be social enemies, have ended up working with each other and trusting each other through their mutual commitment to a life of beggary and vulnerability.

Just as shocking is another group that has been responding positively to him: prostitutes! He allows them to be present at meals. On one recent occasion he even allowed a prostitute to touch him, washing his feet with her hair—in the house of a Pharisee, no less! You can imagine the offense this created for the host. This incident set back Jesus's attempt to enlist the support of the Pharisaic community in Bethsaida. Along with scribes who are educated in the law, some of the Pharisees are the only other ones able to see the moral inconsistencies and dangerous tendencies in Jesus's message and actions.

I believe we will be returning soon to the tetrarchy of Herod.

Despite the insanities of our time, God will prevail. Peace.

X

RATHER THAN MAKING A complete circuit around Lake Galilee, which would have meant going through a number of largely Gentile towns, Jesus arranged for some fishing boats to take us across to Magdala. By now, hundreds of people wanted to follow Jesus—at least for a day or two—so it was a small fleet that crossed the lake, and those who couldn't acquire passage simply rushed around the lake on foot to meet us on the other side. By the time we got to Magdala it was late in the afternoon, and the crowds that had traveled by foot had swelled in number and were exhausted. Some of the Twelve suggested to Jesus that he ought to send everyone home or tell them to find places to eat. Jesus became lost in thought for a while, and then announced, "No, let's have a meal with everyone right here."

The jaws of the Twelve dropped. Rock asked, "How are we going to feed a crowd of this size?"

Jesus asked, "How much food do we have with us?"

Philip, who was in charge of food supplies, looked through his bag and said, "A boy this morning gave us five loaves of bread and two dried fish. That's all we've got."

Jesus nodded. "Tell everyone to sit down. Divide them into twelve groups, like the twelve tribes of Israel. You're going to serve them a great meal."

The field outside Magdala was a pleasant spot, full of green grass. The crowd reclined on the cushioned ground in twelve clusters with more than a hundred people in each cluster. Jesus then took the five loaves and two fish, looked into the sky, and loudly—triumphantly—thanked God:

"Abba! May your name be honored everywhere! May your reign come upon us now! Provide us with the bread we need today, and deliver us from all that is evil!"

He then broke the bread, handed it to the Twelve, and told them to give each group a piece. He split apart the fish and had them distribute it in the same way.

As tiny morsels of food passed from hand to hand, we couldn't help but be reminded of the time of our ancestors, when God had fed them in the wilderness, providing them with manna from heaven, enough for each day. It was now happening again. People began weeping with joy; others started singing songs of God's deliverance; some people mimicked stuffing food in their mouths, drinking flasks of wine, and then patted their stomachs with satisfaction. Laughter broke out. A party began.

I can't really say what happened, but suddenly there was a lot more food. I suppose people were sharing with each other whatever they might have had with them. In any case, we celebrated as if God's manna was all around us and God's pillar of smoke and fire was leading us faithfully through the wilderness and into the promised land of abundance and freedom. As those peasants munched on crumbs, visions filled their faces and tears streamed down their cheeks. It was a dream Jesus had conjured for them.

But only a dream.

XI

FOR TWO DAYS WE walked to Nazareth, a village of about two hundred people. Far from Lake Galilee, as well as the Great Sea, it was a hamlet of small farms, vineyards, and orchards, and the home of Jesus's family of stonecutters and carpenters who supplied materials for nearby Sepphoris. When Jesus arrived in town followed by the Twelve and a sundry assortment of disciples who strained the meager resources of Nazareth, the townsfolk were clearly happier to see Jesus than to see us. Nevertheless, there was much hugging and kissing of cheeks for all of us, as well as a sheep slaughtered for his village-wide homecoming party.

The following evening the Sabbath began, so the next morning we all crowded into a little synagogue. After prayers were offered and Scriptures read, the oldest member of the community invited Jesus to speak. Seated where everyone could see him, Jesus announced to the folks he had grown up with that God's empire was now dawning; he invited them to share their resources with all who were in need, trust in God, and join him in his mission to spread the good news. But even though Jesus was using the same words I had heard him speak in many other places, the dazzle was missing, and the response was an embarrassing silence. People looked down at their feet or took a sudden interest in the ceiling beams. The elderly leader gave a benediction, and everyone began dispersing.

Outside I overheard one man say to another, "Who does he think he is? He's a carpenter. He's Mary's son." The other person grunted assent.

I thought it odd that the man referred to Jesus as "Mary's son." Why wasn't he identified by his father's name? Was his father long dead? Was there a question about his paternity?

Someone else said to a neighbor, "Every traveler coming through here claims Jesus has the power to heal illnesses and cast out demons. He never did that while he lived here." The neighbor agreed it was just hype.

We spent another day in Nazareth. I met Jesus's brothers: James, Joses, Judas, and Simon. They all struck me as staid, pious, and unimaginative. I met his sisters too: all very quiet. Unless Jesus's personality had undergone a transformation since he left home, he must have stuck out like a sore thumb in his family while he was growing up. I noticed that most of the villagers avoided his home while we were there, and no one ever came for healing. It was extraordinary to see Jesus reduced to a misfit peasant. These people knew him: they had taught him, played with him, worked with him, watched him grow up, knew every aspect of his personality and every little thing he had ever done. He wasn't a great prophet and healer. He was just Jesus.

Jesus was obviously uncomfortable and troubled by everyone's lack of response to his message. His family was kind to him and glad to have him home, but it seemed clear to me they were hoping to find a way to protect him from his own delusions and make him normal.

While in Nazareth, I was struck by something missing: his wife. Was Jesus widowed? Had he never married? I found it strange that a man of his age would have no wife. I managed to sidle up to him, outside of others' hearing, and ask him, "Are you not married?"

He looked away and said, "Some men are born eunuchs, some have been made eunuchs by others, and some have made themselves eunuchs for the sake of God's empire."

What kind of eunuch was he? I wasn't sure how to interpret this enigmatic remark and decided to drop the matter.

On the day following the Sabbath, I saw Jesus looking sadly at a woman sitting by herself in the dust: unkempt, rocking back and forth, muttering incomprehensible words. She was probably a woman he had known all his life. He walked over to her, bent down, placed a gentle hand on her shoulder, and whispered in her ear. She demonstrated no sign of recognition; her rocking and muttering continued. Jesus turned away, his head bowed.

It occurred to me that I ought to make a quick trip to nearby Sepphoris to visit my wife and daughter. But what could I tell my wife I was doing? I decided I better not risk making a visit. Jesus was so unpredictable, he might leave Nazareth at any moment, and if I wasn't going to keep my hand to the plow he would have no hesitancy leaving me behind.

The morning we left town was a relief for everyone—the villagers, his family, we disciples, and even Jesus. Seeking to rehabilitate himself in our eyes, Jesus said to us on the road, "Prophets find honor, except in their hometowns, among their relatives, and in their own homes."

Who sees you more clearly: your family and friends who have known you since you were a child, or those who have only witnessed your unfolding as an adult? Is any prophet respected by their family? If not, is it because no one is truly a prophet? Or perhaps even the greatest prophet is always, at the same time, simply someone's son or daughter, an ordinary sibling or spouse.

As we walked ever farther from Nazareth, I pondered the lack of faith and wonders. Jesus's message seemed to work only if you believed it. But does believing make it true?

XII

AFTER HIS DISCOURAGEMENT IN Nazareth, Jesus returned to Capernaum where he had previously generated large, enthusiastic crowds. We stayed at the house of Rock's mother-in-law, which had the benefit of a courtyard and a couple of storage buildings. Even so, accommodations for all of us were tight, and every day a mass of townspeople filled the house and courtyard to listen to Jesus's preaching. It made meals difficult and privacy impossible.

On the second day, while Jesus was teaching in the house, dirt and turf started falling from the ceiling. Suddenly a chunk of roof was pulled away revealing a big gap filled with blue sky. At this point even Jesus couldn't keep the attention of the crowd. Everyone looked up in shock as a man on a stretcher was lowered by ropes handled by four men on the roof. Initially I felt outrage that these people had torn up the roof to get to Jesus, but then I recognized the desperation displayed by their actions.

One of the four men shouted down at Jesus, "Heal him, teacher! Our friend lost the ability to use his legs. Help him!"

Jesus squeezed his way to the middle of the room, looked up at the hole in the roof, looked down at the man lying on the stretcher, and broke out laughing. His chest heaved, he slapped his knee, and tears streamed down his cheeks. As if an emotional dam had burst, his convulsions of glee gushed out, and for a long time the whole crowd joined him in laughter. Finally, he let out a sigh, wiped his eyes with his knuckles, looked at the man on the stretcher, and with a big grin on his face he said, "Son, all your sins are forgiven!"

Up to this point I'd been smiling while Jesus laughed. But when he pronounced forgiveness on this man, my smile disappeared. Jesus had just committed the heresy of John the Baptizer. Two years before, the Baptizer violated the sanctity of the law, the temple, and the priesthood by presuming that he, on his own initiative, could wash away the sins of Israel in the Jordan River. Now Jesus was repeating the Baptizer's impertinence. If Jesus was merely forgiving these men for tearing up the roof, that would be understandable and gracious (though it was not Jesus's roof!). Instead, Jesus was pronouncing complete forgiveness. Is Jesus the high priest? Has a sacrifice been made? Are we in the temple? Is this the Day of Atonement? At least the Baptizer had the moral dignity to require confession of sin and a commitment to change, but even that was missing! On what possible basis could Jesus claim to forgive this man?

Jesus caught my eye. He surveyed the room and then said to all of us, "Which is easier? To forgive or to heal?"

The question seemed illogical to me. One is not easier than the other; instead, they are linked. As soon as this thought went through my head, I realized where Jesus was going with this.

"To show you I have God's authority to forgive sins," Jesus then paused and looked at the man on the stretcher, "I'm telling you: stand up, take your stretcher, and go home."

The man's body jerked, and then to my astonishment, he swung his legs off the stretcher. Grinning like a fool, he stood up, lifting his knees, testing each leg. The crowd roared, shouting praises to God. People clapped and sang psalms of deliverance. While the whooping and singing continued, the man untied the ropes from the stretcher, held the stretcher over his head, and then walked through the crowd and out the door. I had never seen anything like it. Most of Jesus's healings were internal, subjective, impossible to see visually. But unless this was some elaborately staged trick (and I thought through what would have been required to pull it off), the man was visibly, physically restored. I can describe it, but I can't explain it.

After that, a surge of energy was palpable in Capernaum. The next Sabbath, while Jesus was worshiping in the synagogue, an old man approached him whose right hand was clenched, his fingers gnarled and stiff.

"Teacher," he pleaded, "heal my hand. It's useless and painful."

Since this was the Sabbath, a day of holy rest, I expected Jesus to tell the man to come around to Rock's house at sundown for healing. Instead, Jesus asked everyone in the synagogue, "Is it lawful to do good on the Sabbath? If a man has a sheep that falls in a ravine on the Sabbath, won't he pull it out? I'm telling you now: human beings were not made for the benefit of the Sabbath; the Sabbath was made for the benefit of human beings."

He then turned to the old man. "I tell you, stretch out your hand."

Slowly the man's fingers uncurled and spread apart. I was as surprised by his disregard for Sabbath rest as I was by the healing. Did he think he had the authority, on his own, to decide what is lawful on the Sabbath? I was happy for the old man but offended by Jesus. Presuming to possess, on one's own, the authority to interpret the most sacred laws is indistinguishable from making up one's own rules.

After a week in Capernaum, conditions became intolerable. We were never left alone. The crowd was always pressing, always wanting, always hungry for more. Jesus didn't have the heart to tell them to leave. Seeing how harassed and helpless their lives were, he said the crowd was like starving sheep without a shepherd. They needed feeding and tender care to make them strong. But was his constant attention for them also feeding his need for their attention? The whole situation seemed to be spiraling out of control.

Not all of the attention he was receiving was positive. His pronouncements of forgiveness, as well as healing on the Sabbath, had drawn the scrutiny of scribes from Jerusalem, and it created a backlash from the leader of the synagogue. Religious leaders began heckling him in the marketplace and challenging his authority. One scribe interrupted Jesus while he was teaching by shouting,

"He's possessed by Beelzebul, the prince of demons! That's the source of his power!"

Anger flared in Jesus's eyes as I had never seen before. He pushed through the crowd and got right in the face of the scribe. "How can grapes grow from thistles? How can good sprout from evil? How can Satan cast out Satan? His empire would be divided and fall. If it is by the finger of God that I cast out demons then know that God's empire has come upon you—right here, right now!"

Later that day, when we were back in the house of Rock's mother-in-law and the crowd once again jammed the room and the courtyard, a verbal message was passed from person to person from outside to inside and delivered to Jesus: "Your mother and brothers are outside and want you to come out to speak with them."

Jesus sent a simple verbal message back out to his family: "What about?"

A little while later another verbal message was passed back in: "They're concerned about you. People are saying you don't have time to eat and rest and you've become unwell. Your family wants to take you home and take care of you."

I felt badly for Jesus as well as his family. He was indeed being overwhelmed by demands and criticism, and he was looking haggard. But after listening to the humiliating message, Jesus scanned the packed room and asked, "Who's my mother? Who are my brothers? You are. You're my family now. Whoever does the will of God is my brother, my sister, my mother."

> Caleb the scribe to Theodorus:
>
> I congratulate the government on finally sending representatives to confront Jesus's outrageous claims of authority in matters of the law. The better educated and informed segments of the population are taking a stand against him. He is no longer given automatic deference in the synagogues.
>
> Jesus is also facing internal dissention. His hometown has snubbed him, and he has now publicly disowned his family.

But this has not stopped enthusiastic support from a large number of the common people in Capernaum.

Though he rails against an unjust system, he so far has made no direct verbal attacks against the government. He is careful to keep his political statements vague enough to avoid arrest. At this point it is hard for me to discern which way the wind is going to blow. I will keep you posted on any new developments.

For the good of the people, I pray.

XIII

THE NEXT MORNING, BEFORE dawn, Jesus somehow escaped from the house without anyone knowing. When Rock woke up and realized Jesus was gone, he and James and John tried to tiptoe through the dozing masses to track him down. Inevitably, several others awoke and joined the search. Rock found Jesus outside of town, in the hills overlooking Lake Galilee.

"Everyone's looking for you," Rock told him.

"It's time to move on," Jesus responded.

Later that morning we arrived in Chorazin and immediately Jesus received terrible news from the mayor: "John the Baptizer has been beheaded by order of Herod Antipas."

Jesus was jolted. So was I. John was unquestionably the most popular person in the country. His moral fearlessness and integrity were recognized by all, even if religious leaders disparaged his message and methods. His frank condemnation of Herod's marriage to his brother's former wife was shocking, but it won him the open admiration of the peasantry and the secret admiration of the religious leaders. His preaching of imminent judgment sent shock waves through the kingdom, driving thousands to the Jordan River for baptism, creating a fervently loyal following that dwarfed anything Jesus had so far amassed. I was not surprised Herod had decided to arrest him and move him to a prison far out in the desert to keep him isolated from the people. But to execute him? That could lead to an armed revolt.

After hearing the news, Jesus was silent for a long time. Then he said to us, "Why did you go out to the wilderness to the Jordan

43

River? To see a reed shaken by the wind? No. To see a prophet? Yes! And more than a prophet. I tell you, among all those ever born, no one has ever been greater than John. Until now, God's empire has been thwarted by violence, and violent men have attempted to seize it. But now it is dawning. All the law and the prophets have foretold this moment. This is the turning point of the ages."

This may well have been the turning point, but not the one Jesus was expecting. Violent men weren't going to stop now.

That night as we reclined at dinner in the home of a man marked by skin disease (Jesus had dared to touch him and declare him clean), Jesus was in a contemplative mood. He said little until someone asked him about his own experience with the Baptizer.

"Even in Nazareth I had heard of this prophet who demanded that everyone repent of their selfishness and be baptized before the coming of the Messiah. In my spirit I felt summoned to the Jordan River. I left my carpenter shop in the hands of my brothers and traveled to the Jordan River where it spills into the Dead Sea. It is a hot and barren land, a place to be stripped of all that is old and be made new.

"I listened to John, enraptured. He said God's winnowing fork is in his hand, ready to clear the threshing floor, separating the wheat from the chaff, so the wheat could be bagged and the chaff burned. He told the priests from Jerusalem that being the descendants of Abraham wouldn't protect them. 'God is able to turn these stones into Abraham's children!' he said. He demanded complete commitment to God's justice. He told the tax collectors to stop cheating people, and soldiers to stop extorting people, and religious people to stop pretending to be good and instead actually do good.

"Listening to him, I felt compelled to begin a new life dedicated entirely to God alone, so I stepped into the water. Every muscle, every bone, trembled in my body. Something from God was about to happen. John placed his hands on my head and pushed me down into the water. He held me under until I could no longer hold my breath, until I thought I would die. I did die. Then he pulled me up. As the water ran down my face, and I gasped for breath, I saw the sky rip open, revealing God's heaven above it. From heaven came a dove soaring from God's presence and landing on my head. Then I heard a voice from heaven, like all the torrents of water in the world, say to me, 'You are my son, the beloved one, in whom my soul delights.'

"In that moment I realized who I was. I was not a disciple of John the Baptizer. I was the one who brings God's empire.

"I immediately left John and wandered into the wilderness, eating nothing, only praying, waiting for further visions to guide me. The visions came, along with tests and battles with Satan and his demons and wild beasts. By God's Spirit, I overcame them. I now knew how to accomplish my mission. I was ready."

XIV

WHILE IN CHORAZIN, TWO scribes from Jerusalem once again caught up with Jesus, ready for a theological contest. Little did they realize I was part of their guild, since by that time I looked like another starving peasant. I just observed, curious to see how my occupational brethren would outmaneuver Jesus, exposing him as a deluded fool. Their point of attack was to demand proof of his divine authority to eat with unclean and immoral people, forgive sins, and interpret the law.

"Show us a sign," one of them said as we all sat in the shade of a large thorn tree. "We hear you can heal people, so do it now in front of us. Or make it thunder while the sky is clear."

Jesus waved off the demand with a flick of his hand. Was he refusing because he couldn't do it? Did lack of faith among observers block his ability to heal, as seemed to happen in Nazareth? Was he refusing to perform like a trained bear? Or did he regard this demand as an offense against God's dignity?

The other scribe pressed the issue. Jesus, growing frustrated, responded, "The only sign you'll receive is the sign of Jonah. He warned the people of Nineveh, and the people of Nineveh repented. Will you? On the day of God's judgment, the people of Nineveh will rise from their graves and condemn you. I tell you there's something greater than Jonah here! On the day of judgment, the Queen of Sheba will rise from her grave and condemn you, because she traveled from the ends of the earth to hear the wisdom of Solomon. I tell you there's something greater than Solomon here!"

I was amazed that he thought he was greater than Jonah and Solomon. Did not Jonah convert an entire city of Israel's worst enemies? Was not Solomon the wisest of all men, giving us Scriptures and proverbs inspired by God? But Jesus was making a shrewd point about Jonah and Solomon: wisdom and repentance are greater signs of God's presence than doing wonders.

In that moment I felt a pang of embarrassment that I belonged to the same guild as these scribes. They were so haughty that they made no attempt to understand Jesus or recognize his unique brilliance. Despite my deep skepticism of Jesus's message, I felt an urge to defend him against these stuffed cloaks.

"Maybe signs aren't for creating faith but the result of faith," I said. "It's faith that creates signs, not the other way around."

I was surprised by my words—as were the two scribes. They looked at me with disdain, assuming I was just another uneducated dupe. This made me want to defend Jesus all the more.

Jesus smiled at me and said, "You're not far from God's empire."

My face flushed.

The first scribe made a frontal attack. "Welcoming and eating with sinners proves you yourself are unclean. How dare you presume to speak for God!"

Jesus paused a moment to consider his response. He looked at all of us gathered around him as his face softened into a gentle wistfulness.

"There was a man who had two sons. The younger one said one day, 'Abba, give me my share of the inheritance now.' His father was distressed by such disrespect, but he went ahead and divided his property and gave the younger son his share.

"The younger son traveled to a far country where he squandered all his money on gambling and getting drunk. Then a famine swept the land and he found himself starving and penniless. Desperate, he took a job feeding pigs. He was paid so poorly he wanted to eat from the slop given to the pigs, but no one gave him anything. Finally he came to his senses. He said to himself, 'My father's hired hands have plenty to eat while I'm here starving to death. I'll go home and tell my father, "Abba, I have sinned against heaven and against you. I am no longer worthy to be called your son. I beg you to treat me like a hired hand."' Then he started on his way home.

"As he approached home, his father saw him coming down the road, and he was filled with compassion and joy. He ran to him, throwing his arms around him and kissing him. His son said, 'Abba, I have sinned against heaven and against you.' But before he could get another word out of his mouth, his father turned to the servants and said, 'Quick, get a robe—the best one—and put it on him. Put the family ring on his finger and sandals on his feet. Get the fatted calf and kill it. We're going to celebrate. This son of mine was dead but is now alive; he was lost but now is found!'

"Meanwhile, the father's elder son was out in the field working. When he returned home that evening he heard music and dancing going on inside the house. He asked one of the servants what was going on, and the servant replied, 'Your brother has come home, and your father killed the fatted calf because he's now safe and sound.' The elder brother became furious and refused to enter the house.

"The father came outside and pleaded with his son to come in, but his son said, 'Listen! All these years I've worked like a slave for you and I've never disobeyed you, yet you've never given me and my friends so much as a goat for a party. But when this son of yours comes back after wasting a fortune on prostitutes, you kill the fatted calf for him!'

"The father replied, 'Son, you're always with me and all I have is yours. But we had to celebrate, because this brother of yours was dead and is now alive; he was lost but now is found.'"

Everyone was silent as we contemplated this story. I didn't have to ask Jesus what this parable meant. I got it. We scribes are the elder son who never rebels against God but dutifully obeys his every command. But we are filled with resentment and envy toward those who fail to obey. We are especially upset if they repent and receive forgiveness because they had hedonistic fun while we worked. We demand full punishment for every illicit pleasure they experienced, enough misery to wipe out all forbidden gratification. For us, that's God's justice. But for Jesus, God's justice is finding a way for everyone to be healed and redeemed.

That evening, as we ate a meager meal in the home of a day laborer, I asked Jesus, "So how does that story end? Does the elder son come in or not?"

"I don't know," he replied. "We will have to wait and see."

"I hope the elder son joins the party," I said.

"I do too. But I'm afraid he will instead pick up a stick and beat his father."

I pondered that scenario somberly.

"To tell you the truth," he continued, "it's easier for God to save sinners than the righteous."

The next day, while Jesus's critics appeared to be elsewhere, some people brought to him a young man who was blind and begged him to touch him. Jesus put his finger to his lips and glanced around, as if making sure his critics were not watching, and then beckoned them to follow him. He walked straight out of town, followed by a handful of us disciples, townspeople, and the blind man. When he was satisfied no one from Jerusalem was watching, he turned and looked at the young man whose chin held wisps of the first growth of a beard. He seemed to ponder for a moment what to do and then spat in the man's eyes. Closing the man's eyelids with his fingertips, Jesus kept them closed for a while. Then he lifted his fingers and told him to open his eyes.

"Do you see anything?"

The youth looked around, blinking rapidly. "I can see people, but they look like trees."

Jesus placed his fingertips on the man's closed eyelids again and then released him.

"Now what do you see?"

The fellow stared with astonishment. "I see everything!"

XV

ONE NIGHT OUR HOST was a man named Simon, burly and almost toothless. As Jesus talked at the supper table about God's empire overthrowing the devil's empire, Simon grew animated.

"That's right! It's time to overthrow those devils, the Romans!" he shouted with disgust. Then, realizing he had better be careful not to be overheard, he noted under his breath, "I used to run with a gang of bandits. We robbed rich merchants that are sucking our country dry." His weak eyes glittered at the memories, and then he added, "I still have contacts. Let me know if you want me to organize a raid to break into the storehouses of the local landowners."

Jesus shook his head slightly. Slowly, weighing his words, he responded, "That is not how God's empire overthrows the devil. You've been taught to love your friends and hate your enemies. But I tell you, love your enemies."

Simon's head snapped back. "What do you mean?"

"I mean: do good to those who hate you, bless those who curse you, pray for those who abuse you."

Simon's jaw dropped. "That's ridiculous! If we do that, the oppression continues! The rich and powerful will keep their riches and power, and the poor and powerless will continue to suffer."

"Has your way stopped the oppression?" asked Jesus. "Is there less evil in the world because you robbed and killed?"

Simon was silent.

"If someone slaps you on the cheek, insulting you, don't slap them back. Instead, surprise your enemy. Offer your other cheek.

By responding with calm goodness, you refuse to be sucked into an escalation of retaliation."

Jesus let the image sink in for a moment and then continued. "If a landowner takes you to court and sues you because of your unpaid debts, and he takes away your cloak, leaving you cold and miserable, don't take revenge on him. Expose his pitiless greed by stripping off the rest of your clothes and handing them to him—right there in court. Wake up his conscience with your generosity."

With his usual quick thinking, Jesus immediately offered a third image. "If a Roman soldier forces you to carry his pack for a mile, don't grumble and curse him, filling your heart with bitterness and violence. Carry his pack a second mile. The first mile you are his slave, but the second mile you are his brother. By doing good in the face of evil, we change the relationship with our enemies. We change the heart—ours as well as, perhaps, theirs."

Simon's face turned red. "That's foolishness! Are you suggesting we should put ourselves in a position to be slapped again, stripped naked, further humiliated, and do it with a smile? It's bad enough to be treated like a rug; it's worse to say, 'Step on me!'"

"I am not saying to invite abuse. I am saying to use surprising goodness to change the relationship," answered Jesus. "Treat others—even enemies—the way you would want to be treated. If we love only those who love us, how does that change anything? Everyone already does that. If we do good only to those who do good to us, how does that change anything? Even Gentiles do that. But if we love our enemies—doing good to those who insult us, praying for those who harm us—we become the children of God, reflecting God's character. Look: God makes sunlight shine on the noble and the despicable, and God sends rain to water the fields of those who do wrong and those who do right. God showers love without discrimination. When we reflect love the way God loves, God's empire increases. We must be merciful as God is merciful."

On the lips of anyone else, I think Simon would have tossed that person out of his house. But Jesus's words sprang from a place so deep within himself, a place we all long to find within ourselves, that Simon remained silent and contemplative.

As the evening wore on, Jesus and Simon turned aside to speak privately. I caught bits of their conversation, enough to realize that mixed with Simon's gleeful memories of banditry were also traumatic memories of guilt and shame that had haunted him like demons.

The next morning, Simon left his house and came with us, becoming a disciple. That next night, when we were sleeping in a small barn, scrunched together, I noted the irony that Simon the bandit was snoring side by side with Levi the tax collector—enemies in a former life.

Caleb the scribe to Theodorus:

God's peace be ever with our nation.

I have been listening carefully to Jesus's conversations, public and private, for some months now, and I am convinced that despite his message that God's empire is taking over, he does not practice or advocate violence by his followers. His words about peacemaking are not simply a ruse to keep the authorities at bay while he quietly makes plans for a revolt. He truly believes that love and reconciliation with enemies is the basis of God's empire.

Nevertheless, like the Baptizer, he expects a coming judgment by God in which the greedy will be damned and the generous will be blessed. Such expectations feed fanaticism and delusions. Jesus may be a peacemaker, but I'm not so sure about the crowds who listen to him. Some are eager to lend a hand in bringing God's judgment.

If Jesus were to be arrested, it may be that his movement would peter out. On the other hand, it may be that some peasants, out of anger, would rise in revolt. In light of this, I offer another option: leave Jesus alone so that he may continue to foster love and non-retaliation among the people. The result will be a fanatical movement of deluded but harmless dreamers who pose no direct threat to the government.

Ever serving our God.

XVI

ABOUT A WEEK LATER I was in Magdala's marketplace, helping to purchase food for the disciples, when I saw two Pharisees, one with a strong limp and the other with a brand on his left cheek, walking toward me. I recognized them from Tiberias and froze, terrified they would either verbally abuse me for being a follower of Jesus or expose me as a spy working for Herod. Instead, the one with the limp lowered his voice and asked, "Can you tell us where Jesus of Nazareth is?"

Their demeanor gave me the impression they wanted a discrete conversation with him. Curious, I told them I would take them to him. A few minutes later we were in a private courtyard and I was introducing them to Jesus.

They got directly to the point. The one with the brand said, "Teacher, we have connections with some of those who work for Herod's court. It has come to our attention that Herod plans to arrest you and have you executed. You know that some in our party would perhaps be glad to see this happen, but my friend and I feel differently. You are a righteous man. We urge you to get out of Galilee and out of Herod's territory as soon as possible."

I was stunned and suddenly frightened. I had hoped that my last communication with Theodorus might prevent this very action. I felt pain at the thought that Jesus's movement was about to come to a crashing end.

Jesus was unfazed.

"Go tell that fox I'm healing people and defeating the devil every day, and I'm going to keep doing it right here till I decide it's time to go."

The two Pharisees tried to dissuade him, but it was pointless. They left, clearly worried.

After they had gone, Jesus said to me and his bodyguards, "Watch out for the leaven of Herod."

Despite his bold words to the two Pharisees, Jesus realized Herod was dangerous. For the rest of the day I was constantly looking over my shoulder, expecting Herod's soldiers to charge into view. I did not want to see Jesus arrested. I certainly did not want to see him ending up with his head on a platter like the Baptizer. If that happened, I would have to bear partial responsibility. I felt sick and could not sleep that night.

The next morning I felt relief when Jesus announced it was time to leave Galilee, but I was filled with new fears when he said we were heading to Jerusalem for the Feast of Booths. This was like jumping out of a boiling pot and into the fire. Jerusalem was the headquarters of the chief priests and other religious authorities. They would be less than friendly about Jesus's outlandish pronouncements. More concerning, Jerusalem was within the province of Judea, governed directly by a Roman prefect, Pontius Pilate. The Romans were even more prone to executing prophets than Herod was.

Jesus took us up to a cliff edge overlooking almost the entirety of Lake Galilee. Looking down we could see most of the towns and hill country where we had spent the last few months. As we surveyed the lands on the north end of the lake, Jesus's shoulders shook. I had never seen him cry before. He then sat on his haunches and began rocking back and forth. Following his lead, the Twelve also squatted and began rocking, mimicking Jesus's grief.

Jesus's words caught in his throat: "Judgment is coming to you, Chorazin, and judgment is coming to you, Bethsaida. If the mighty things done in your towns had been done among the Gentiles of Tyre and Sidon, they would've changed their hearts, sitting in sackcloth and ashes. On the day of judgment, Tyre and Sidon will be better off than you.

"And you, Capernaum, do you think you're going to be exalted to heaven? No, you're going down to Hades. Those who reject me are rejecting the one who sent me."

I was dumbstruck. Did Jesus consider his ministry in these three towns a failure? Certainly there were many people—even most, I suppose—who ignored his message or even mocked him. But considerable numbers of people listened to him every day, and hundreds of people found relief from their suffering and hope for their lives. He broke down walls between people who would otherwise never speak to each other. In a few remarkable instances, some changed their lives completely, freely sharing the bounty they had accumulated. Was his mission a failure unless everyone embraced love, inclusion, sharing, and a fearless trust in God? Wasn't this expecting too much?

And did Jesus think he was such a pure and complete conduit of God that rejecting him was tantamount to rejecting God? Don't we all have our own individual personalities and habits that inevitably attract some while repelling others? Aren't we all created differently to like and respond to different things? I had to admit it might be wonderful if we all lived and loved as Jesus did, but there has to be room for skepticism, criticism, and even rejection.

XVII

Jesus was in no rush to get to Jerusalem. The Feast of Booths was still weeks away, so he traveled at a leisurely pace on a circuitous route. Sending the Twelve out in pairs to villages along the way, he told them to arrange meals and lodging for our group, assuring plenty of places and opportunities for Jesus to preach and teach. "We must go to every town in Israel," he told us.

To our surprise, he included the towns of Samaria. All of us were aghast that he expected us to eat and sleep in Samaritan homes. How would we be able to maintain our ritual purity for entering the temple when we arrived in Jerusalem? Samaritans were heretics, following a distorted form of the law passed down from Moses and worshiping God in a separate temple with paganized rituals, an illegitimate priesthood, and bastardized scriptures. But Jesus insisted that "they too are among the lost sheep of the house of Israel." Extending table fellowship to tax collectors and prostitutes was already difficult for me to stomach, but this felt like a fundamental violation of faith.

Now that we were outside the territory of Galilee and the jurisdiction of Herod Antipas, I considered leaving Jesus and his disciples and returning home. Later I often wished I had; it would have saved me much grief.

When Jesus sent out the brothers James and John to arrange accommodations in one of the Samaritan towns, they came back quickly with word that the town, unsurprisingly, would not welcome us since we were on our way to Jerusalem. The two Sons of Thunder suggested to Jesus that he curse the town. "Call down fire from heaven to consume them!" urged John. Jesus brushed them off. "Love your enemies," he reminded them. And then he told this story:

"A man was traveling from Jerusalem to Jericho when he was attacked by bandits, robbed, stripped, beaten, and left for dead. Later a priest came walking along and saw the wounded man covered in blood and groaning on the side of the road. The priest passed by on the other side, afraid of contamination if the wounded man died while the priest was handling him. Later a Levite was traveling through. He also saw the wounded man, but he didn't want to be delayed, and he was afraid the robbers might be setting an ambush, so he hurried on.

"But then came a Samaritan down the road riding on a donkey. When he saw the wounded man, he was filled with pity. He immediately got off of his donkey, bandaged the man's wounds, gave him wine to revive him, placed him on his donkey, and took him to the nearest inn where he continued to care for the man. The next morning he gave the innkeeper two days' pay and told him, 'Take care of this man till he recovers. When I come back this way I'll reimburse you for any additional costs.'

"Which of the three who saw the wounded man do you think is in God's empire?"

John provided the answer glumly, "The one who showed mercy, I suppose?"

Jesus nodded.

All of us were bothered by this story. Did Jesus really think Samaritans could be more compassionate than religious Jews? And did he really think heretics could be part of God's empire?

Another pair of disciples came back from the Samaritan city of Sychar reporting that some of the people in the city were willing to host us. Surprised, we headed to Sychar.

Arriving at midday, the heat was oppressive. Outside of town was a well. Sweating profusely, Jesus sat down under a tamarisk tree by the well and told us to go into Sychar and buy food. We assumed he wanted to be alone to pray, so we left him and headed into town. Our experience in the marketplace was frustrating since it was impossible to know whether some of the food, especially the meat and bread, had been prepared properly. After much haggling, we bought what we thought we would need and returned to Jesus.

When we arrived at the well, we were stunned to see Jesus in conversation with a Samaritan woman. He was even drinking from a gourd she had passed to him. Was there a single tradition for maintaining social and ritual purity that this man did not violate?

The woman, embarrassed by our presence, quickly left, leaving behind her water jug in her hurry. We were also embarrassed, so much so that none of us knew what to say to Jesus. Finally, Rock broke the tension by asking Jesus whether he thought we should eat the bread and meat we had bought in the marketplace since it might not be kosher.

Jesus replied, "Listen to me, all of you: there is nothing from outside a person that, by going into his mouth, defiles him. It doesn't go to his heart; it only goes to his stomach and then out of his body into the sewer. It's what comes out of our mouths—not what comes into our mouths—that defiles us. It is from here," he tapped his heart, "that we are defiled."

I wondered: how seriously does Jesus take the food laws given to us by Moses? He always claimed he upheld the inviolability of Moses's laws. But at the same time, he also told us to accept food offered to us by our hosts in good faith. "Accept it all as a gift from God," he would tell us. Did this apply even to a Samaritan marketplace? When do accommodation, trust, and "good faith" become violations of the law? His extremely loose application of some of Moses's laws continued to unsettle me.

> Caleb the scribe to Theodorus:
>
> May God protect us during these dangerous times.
>
> Jesus was tipped off that Herod was planning to arrest him, so he has now left Galilee and is currently in Samaria. We will soon be in Judea, and then in Jerusalem for the Feast of Booths.
>
> Jesus is demonstrating extraordinary cooperation with the Samaritans and is trying to recruit them into his movement. His appeal, so far, is limited, but it is

concerning if he succeeds in joining the discontent of the Galilean peasantry with the rebellious Samaritans.

Since Jesus is no longer in Herod's territory, do you wish me to continue my surveillance? I would welcome a return home and to my scribal duties.

Ever faithful.

Theodorus to Caleb:

Continue to monitor Jesus in Judea since he may return to Galilee after the Feast of Booths. Your bank account is swelling.

Destroy this message after reading. God protect you.

XVIII

WE WERE STAYING IN a Jewish home on the border of Samaria and Judea when a woman came to the house and, from outside, asked if Jesus could come out to speak to her. Jesus came to the doorway. Even he was surprised when he saw that she was neither a Jew nor a Samaritan. Based on the fabric and dyes of her clothing, she was evidently a Syrophoenician—a Gentile!

As soon as he came to the doorway, she bowed down to the ground and begged Jesus to come to her home and drive a demon out of her daughter who was sick in bed. Jesus seemed hesitant about what to do. As far as I knew, he had never been approached by a Gentile for help. How had she heard about him, I wondered, or known where he was staying? It was all quite confusing and uncomfortable.

For all of us, it was clear what Jesus had to do: send her away. God may have mercy on a God-fearing Gentile, but Gentiles are not a part of the household of Israel. Jesus felt the same way, telling her, "Let the children be fed first. It's not fair to take the children's bread and throw it outside to the dogs."

I was relieved to see Jesus finally drawing a line and making necessary distinctions. Gentiles, like dogs, are unclean. We can be kind to them, work out peaceable arrangements with them, but we don't include them in the holiness of our daily lives. As Jesus suggested, they are not the appropriate focus of his ministry to redeem Israel. We can't help everyone. We all have to maintain boundaries or we achieve nothing.

After Jesus's firm response, I fully expected the woman to leave. Instead, she lifted her face from the ground, looked directly into Jesus's face, and had the impertinence to disagree with him. "Sir, in my country the dogs aren't outside. We keep them in the house because they are loyal and helpful. They rest under the table and eat the crumbs that the children drop for them."

Jesus's eyes welled up with tears. Quietly he responded, "Go on home. The demon is now driven from your daughter."

She bowed again in gratitude, accepting his pronouncement as true, and hurried off. At first, I couldn't figure out whether Jesus had employed a ruse to get rid of her or whether he actually believed he had healed a girl he had never seen. If he was being sincere about pronouncing healing for the girl, had it worked? If it had been possible, I would have followed the Gentile woman to her home to find out.

But more perturbing was the fact that Jesus had given in to this woman. I had often seen him bend like grass to help someone who should not have been helped. But this was the first time I saw him take a stand and then change his mind. And it was a Gentile woman who caused it.

A week later we arrived in Bethany, a small town a couple of miles from the walls of Jerusalem on the other side of the Mount of Olives. Jesus accepted an invitation to dinner in the home of a wealthy widow, Martha. As we waited for the food to be served, we sat in the dining area while Jesus expounded on God's empire to a variety of local guests. Then, to my amazement, Martha's younger sister, Mary, sat down with the men to listen to Jesus. I looked at Jesus. He didn't bat an eye as he continued his teaching, despite everyone's embarrassment.

We weren't the only ones embarrassed. Martha came bustling into the room, her face red. "I apologize, sir, for my sister's behavior. She's left me all alone in preparing the meal. Please instruct her to assist me."

Instead, Jesus smiled and replied, "Dear Martha, you're so worried and upset! Calm down. Only one thing truly matters, and your sister, Mary, has found it. I'm not going to take that away from her."

Once again Jesus swept aside the proper social boundaries between men and women. I could only shake my head. From then on, Jesus made a point of having dinner at Martha's house as often as possible whenever we were near Jerusalem. In addition to his obvious fondness for the sisters, he may have seen the location of their home as fortuitous. Being close to Jerusalem, but not in Jerusalem, gave him access to the temple and the city during the day while also giving him a safe retreat at night with an easy escape to the surrounding hills in case the authorities came after him.

XIX

IF YOU'VE NEVER BEEN to Jerusalem, you've never seen the greatest wonder in the world: the temple built by Herod the Great. If one stands on the top of the Mount of Olives, gazing downward across the Kidron Valley at the temple resting on top of the highest hill of Jerusalem, it shines like a pearl, its polished white marble walls and gold accents reflecting the sun's rays across the massive courtyard and across the entire city. After entering the city from the south, one approaches an edifice of massive blocks of stone, provoking awe, each one chiseled and embossed to perfection. Ascending a broad stairway through the double Huldah gates, one continues through a tunnel until emerging in the largest plaza in the country, surrounded by pillared porticos and dominated at the far end by the gleaming temple. Moving to the right across the open plaza and then approaching the Beautiful Gate to the inner courtyard, which only Jewish men may enter, one is dazzled by the majesty of the face of the temple. Going through the gate and across the inner courtyard past the smoking altar of sacrifice, one is confronted by two gigantic pillars, Boaz and Jachin, guarding the entrance to the temple. If one is a Levite or priest, one may pass through the entrance into the temple itself, where the roof soars above while below one's feet the floor glistens with colored marble fitted together in geometric patterns. Directly ahead is the curtain behind which is the Holy of Holies, the very place where the high priest encounters the glory of God on the Day of Atonement. It is hard to imagine that in all the world there could be a more magnificent building.

During the Feast of Booths, we entered the massive plaza beside the temple every day. Jesus always headed for Solomon's Portico, a lengthy, shaded place where rabbis debated and the religious council—the Sanhedrin—met to make its decisions. Meeting with the rabbis, Jesus discussed the law with them. One day the topic turned to divorce.

A Pharisee posed a question that was often debated: "Is it lawful for a man to divorce his wife for any cause?"

The issue was contentious since Moses was vague about the proper grounds for divorce, only saying that a man may write his wife a certificate of divorce if he finds something objectionable about her. But what constitutes objectionable? The illustrious Rabbi Shammai believed this referred to a serious transgression, such as adultery, whereas the equally renowned Rabbi Hillel took the position that the husband could divorce his wife for something as trivial as overcooking the supper. I was curious which position Jesus would favor. It turned out the answer was neither.

"Haven't you read that, in the beginning, God made human beings male and female, and that he ordained the man to leave his father and mother and cling to his wife, and that the two therefore become one? If God has joined a man and woman together as one, no one ought to separate them."

The Pharisee raised an objection. "Then why did Moses say a man could give his wife a certificate of divorce?"

"Moses said this as a concession to the hard-heartedness of men, but this is not God's will. Divorcing your wife and marrying another is legalized adultery."

Everyone within earshot under the portico let out a gasp. This was too much even for those of us following Jesus. James blurted out, "If we're stuck with our wives no matter what, it's better not to get married at all!"

As I later pondered his words, I began to see that Jesus was calling on men to make their marriages more honorable. The prophet Micah declared that God hated divorce, that we should love the wife of our youth. Divorce, which forces a woman out of her home without any recourse, separating her from her own children, plunges her into destitution—even prostitution—since most men refuse to marry a divorced woman. How many men got rid of their wives in order to marry someone younger and prettier? I found Jesus's vision for marriage admirable and pure, but ironic given the fact that he appeared not to have a wife himself.

But are there not times when marriage becomes intolerable, when divorce does less harm than a continued marriage? Jesus admitted that Moses's law of divorce is a concession. We are indeed hard-hearted.

Jesus quickly got a reputation in Jerusalem for radical interpretations of the law emphasizing compassion and reconciliation. Crowds began to gather around these discussions, and the less educated appreciated the way he stood up to the religious authorities. One morning he was engaged in a long debate with the rabbis about whether we should ever pass a judgment of condemnation on others.

"Do not judge," he told them, "or God will judge you. Do not condemn, or God will condemn you. The judgment you give is the judgment you'll receive, and the condemnation you give is the condemnation you'll receive. But the mercy you give is the mercy you'll receive, and the forgiveness you give is the forgiveness you'll receive."

About an hour later a cluster of scribes brought a case to test his assertions. Two of them held a distraught woman by her arms.

"Teacher, this woman was caught in the act of adultery. Moses's law says such a woman is to be stoned to death. What do you say?"

I wondered how they managed to find an adulterous woman so conveniently for refuting what Jesus had just taught. It was a neat trap. If he agreed she ought to be executed, it would undermine his teaching and he would lose credibility. If he said she should not be executed, he could be accused of violating Moses's law, possibly resulting in a fine, or even a flogging during these highly polarized times.

Jesus crouched down and doodled in the dust. Was he ignoring their question, refusing to give it the dignity of an answer? Or was he stalling for time? Either way, the group of scribes smelled blood. Their trap was tightening, so they kept pressing Jesus for an answer, taunting him. Jesus continued scribbling, seemingly unperturbed, and then stopped, straightened up, and looked directly at each one of the scribes.

"Whoever is without sin, throw the first stone," he said softly.

Then he bent down again, drawing figures in the dirt, as if the matter was settled.

I could imagine one of these pompous scribes (yes, some scribes are indeed pompous) picking up a stone right then and there and throwing it full force at the cringing woman. But Jesus's calmness and sincerity had a way of disarming people. I noticed that when he challenged people, he did not back them into a corner, provoking their instinct to fight. Instead, he gave them an opening for their own choices.

The eldest of the scribes, a man with a grizzled, gray beard and a patch over one eye, turned and walked away. Gradually the other scribes did the same.

I thought about Jesus's response. He did not question the law of execution; he questioned whether we were morally fit to carry it out. I appreciated the creativity and sensitivity he brought to interpreting the law. But did he have the authority to discern the true heart of God? And how could such interpretations be codified and carried out by courts? His approach, as always, was a dream.

After the group of scribes left, Jesus stood up again and asked the woman, "Have any of them condemned you?"

The shamed woman trembled. "No, sir."

"I don't condemn you either. Go home, but don't sin again."

Jesus saved her from execution but not from responsibility. He was merciful but uncompromising, forgiving but demanding. Somehow he held contradictions together.

As the rays of the dying sun flooded Solomon's Portico, Jesus concluded his teaching with a story: "A man planted a fig tree in his vineyard. Year after year he waited for it to produce figs, but it failed each year. He told his gardener, 'I've been looking for figs on this tree for three years now and have found none. It's wasting good soil. It's time to cut it down.' But the gardener pleaded with him, 'Sir, leave it alone for one more year. I'll dig around it and put manure on it. If it's still barren next year, I'll cut it down.'"

One more year. That's all the time Jesus saw left for the people of Israel. Based on the response I was seeing in Jerusalem, maybe the figs were coming. The crowds, a mix of Galilean pilgrims and a diverse collection of local inhabitants, were enthusiastic and typically larger than what I had seen in Galilee. And he now had a new and very promising disciple. Because of a recent defection among the Twelve, Jesus filled the vacancy with a property manager from Jerusalem named Judas. A new recruit, Jesus gave him the nickname "City Man" since he was more urbanized than the rest of us. Because of his financial background, he was given the job of being the group treasurer, carrying the communal money bag. He impressed everyone with his ease around people and his knowledge of the politics in Jerusalem.

One afternoon while Jesus was taking a nap under an awning, Judas said to me, "Let's buy some fish for tonight." I followed him down an alley until I realized we weren't headed to the fish monger; he simply wanted to get me away from the other disciples.

"So Caleb, where are you from?"

"Sepphoris."

"Sepphoris! That's a beautiful little city! Antipas did a great job rebuilding it. I understand it was a heap of ruins after the rebellion there thirty years ago."

"Yes, it has many fine homes now. The amphitheater is particularly beautiful."

"You surprise me! I wouldn't have thought a scribe would approve of worldly entertainment."

I blushed. "I haven't actually attended any dramas, but I admire the architecture."

"I'm not sure I believe you," he whispered with a smile. "So what's a scribe from a fine city doing following this band of country bumkins?"

When he saw my look of shock, he hurriedly added, "I'm not referring to Jesus, of course. He's impressive. But I'm sure you must find these other peasants a bit embarrassing."

I smiled but didn't say anything. It was a relief to be with someone with whom I had something in common.

Judas's eyes narrowed as he asked, "You're not a spy, are you?"

I sputtered, trying to find the right tone of indignation.

"Don't worry!" he laughed. "Your secret is safe with me."

"I'm not a spy! That's a terrible thing to say!"

He laughed some more. "I'm only kidding you."

Our walk through the streets and alleys of Jerusalem continued for some time as we continued to talk about our families and backgrounds. Despite the panic he caused me with his joke about my being a spy, the longer we talked, the longer I felt comfortable with him. I didn't tell him what I really thought about Jesus and his mission, but here was someone with the kind of education and knowledge of the world that I had been missing for months. From that day on, we often hung out together. Since he was part of that special inner circle of the Twelve, being in his presence gave me a sense of also being an insider. I was important.

Caleb the scribe to Theodorus:

God save the people.

Jesus is now in Jerusalem and spends each day under Solomon's Portico in discussion with the rabbis and scribes. A recent healing of a paralyzed man at the Bethzatha Pool has rapidly increased his reputation and popularity. Large numbers of pilgrims have been listening to him, but also the local population. This includes the more educated Greek-speakers. Quite distinct from the ordinary peasantry, these Greek speakers are resourceful and well traveled. It is surprising to see Jesus making inroads among them. One has even become part of his inner circle of disciples.

I believe Jesus's plan is to leave Jerusalem soon but remain in the Judean territory, building up his movement in this area. Jericho is likely our next destination, though it is hard to know since Jesus makes his plans one day at a time. I expect we will return to Jerusalem for the Passover Festival in a few months.

The Sanhedrin has no love for Jesus but has not made any moves against him other than debating him through intermediaries. Likewise, the Roman government is leaving him alone for now. Doubtless, Pontius Pilate has his own spies and is keeping an eye on Jesus.

May God's truth become evident.

XX

AFTER LEAVING JERUSALEM, WE did indeed go to Jericho, where Jesus had success in reforming the rapacious policies of a tax collector named Zacchaeus. Impressed by the tax collector's commitment to give away half his wealth and make generous reparations to those whom he had defrauded, Jesus announced, "Today salvation has come to this house!" Another rich man, on the other hand, walked away from Jesus's invitation to divest himself of his wealth and join God's empire. Jesus took this rejection hard since he had seen great potential in the young man.

While in Jericho, Jesus decided to pair up his itinerant followers and send us out to the various villages of Judea and Perea to pronounce God's healing of the sick, welcome to the outcasts, and good news for the poor: "God's invading empire is here!" We carried nothing with us but the clothes on our backs, trusting that God would open the hearts of the villagers to provide our needs. I was paired up with a talkative tentmaker, which was a relief since that meant I did not have to do the preaching. Being known as disciples of the prophet from Nazareth gave us a kind of aura among the villagers, which often translated into uncommon generosity. Many distressed people said we had brought them relief from their pain, as well as hope for God's new world. I felt deeply conflicted.

A few weeks later we all regrouped in Jericho. Rock and his brother Andrew claimed they had successfully driven out large numbers of demons while on their mission. Jesus, delighted, told them, "I was watching Satan fall like lightning from heaven!"

As the Passover Festival approached, Jesus made plans to return to Jerusalem. The night before leaving Jericho, as we reclined at dinner, Jesus broke the bread, said a prayer, and then announced, "All of those who want to be my disciples must deny themselves and face possible execution. But know this: some of you will not taste death until you've seen God's empire come with power."

Jesus was often enigmatic, but this was ominous. We soaked up his words in silence.

As he took a flask of wine and poured it into a cup, he said, "Among the Gentiles, rulers exert control for their own interests, and the leaders they call 'great' are actually tyrants. That's not how it is among you. Whoever wants to be great must be a servant; whoever wants to rule must be a slave. I came not to be served but to serve, and to give my life as a ransom to free many."

Did Jesus expect this to be the last journey? Was this going to be his death march?

After the dinner, Jesus whispered to me, "Walk with me."

We left the house and walked down a street embedded with small white stones that reflected the light of the moon, offering a softly glowing path to follow. Soon we were on the edge of town, surrounded by dark fields and the sound of crickets.

"Watcher, why do you follow me?"

I shuddered.

"You do not believe what I teach."

I looked down. "I believe some of it."

"Not what matters." He paused. "Who do you think I am?"

"You're a prophet."

"A true prophet?"

I struggled to find an answer. "A true prophet is not known in his own time."

"And yet now we must decide how we will respond," he countered.

"Yes."

"So why do you follow me?"

I took a quick breath and almost told him: I am a spy. It was not my strength that prevented me from telling him, but my cowardice. I sidestepped the question, instead letting my doubts spill out.

"I do not see how God's empire is going to come. We may see it sprout here and there, but it will never take hold. I've heard you say, as David says in the Psalms, that the meek will inherit the earth. Forgive me, but that will never happen. Meekness, kindness, love—they are fine for neighbors and small villages, but they will not stand against armies and kings and the workings of the wider world. We are not good enough, we are not strong enough, and we are not faithful enough to bring God's empire. It won't happen. The only empires that have ever ruled this world were brought with a sword. If God's empire is going to come, it will need an army, and not an army of peasants wielding clubs—that kind of army would be slaughtered. It'll need to be an army of God's angels bringing holy destruction and annihilation on all governments and institutions, because all that we are and all that we've created is full of evil. But I don't pray for that day to come. I pray it will be delayed as long as possible."

He sighed. "You want this world of tears and injustice to continue?"

"It's better than annihilation. I see no other choice."

"Do you believe God will raise us to a new life in a redeemed world?"

"That is beyond my comprehension."

"Indeed." He touched my chest. "But not beyond your heart."

Jesus turned from me and stared into the dark fields. "God's empire is like a farmer who scatters seed on the ground. He sleeps, he rises, he sleeps again, and the seed sprouts and grows—he doesn't know how. The earth grows the seed by itself. First we see the stalk, then we see the head, then we see the full grain in the head. When the grain is ripe, the farmer swings his sickle because it's harvest time."

I shook my head. "You're going to have to chew that one for me."

Jesus smiled. "We cast the seed. We cast hope, generosity, sharing, compassion, forgiveness. But it's God who grows the seed, not us. We don't even know how it happens. We water, but it is God who will bring the harvest, not us. You're right—we aren't good enough or strong enough or faithful enough. So God will do it. When the time is ripe, God will harvest the good grain and all will be God's empire."

"You see wheat," I offered, "but I see weeds. And there are a lot more weeds in this world than wheat."

"I see both," he responded. "And for now they will grow together—the wheat and the weeds—because it's impossible for us to pull out the weeds without pulling out the wheat as well. But if we keep extending mercy, I assure you the wheat will become more bountiful than the weeds. We leave it to God, at harvest time, to do the sorting."

I looked down and muttered, "This world will crush you."

"Yes," he admitted, "and God's love will be crushed too, and often. That is why I am speaking to you. You are not ready. You do not believe. And if you do not believe, you will betray me and you will betray God's empire. You will even betray yourself. Wouldn't it be better to leave now before it's too late?"

My breath was suddenly sucked out of me. I crumpled to my knees and put my face in my hands. I felt the light touch of his fingers on the top of my head. He whispered a prayer and then walked away

XXI

WELL BEFORE THE SUN rose the next morning, speaking to no one, I walked out of Jericho, leaving Jesus and his disciples behind. My plan was to head for Tiberias and tell Theodorus I had been found out and driven away by Jesus. I was done with this spying business.

But I had gone no more than two miles out of the city when I heard groaning down in a gully. I hesitated, afraid of what might be lying in wait in the dark shadows below, but finally stepped off the road and slid down into the wadi. Guided in the semi-darkness by an occasional moan, I found a man sprawled out under some bushes, his hair matted by an enormous clot of dried blood. As I knelt, his eyes flickered opened. Untying a skin of water from my belt, I gently lifted his head and poured a little water between his lips. He drank some, and then a little more. Arms trembling, he tried to sit up. I helped him into a sitting position and then he took a long gulp of water.

I asked him several questions about how he received his injury, but he made no response. He seemed confused and unable to talk, so I never found out what had happened to him. After a while I managed to help him out of the wadi and into a shady spot by the road. Just then, to my surprise and embarrassment, I saw Jesus and the disciples coming down the road. When they saw me sitting with a wounded man, they said nothing to me but immediately stopped to assist the wounded man. After cleaning a gash on his scalp and wrapping his head with a cloth, they shared some food with him. Then Jesus suggested to Philip that he take the unsteady man back to Jericho and find a home where he could recover while

Jesus and the rest of the disciples continued on their way toward Jerusalem. Philip, being young and strong, would have no problem catching up with them.

Philip readily agreed, and soon Jesus and the rest of his followers resumed their journey. Again, they said nothing to me, but I had the sense that some kind of providence was at work. I quietly rejoined them.

I decided to stick with Jesus and his motley band partly because I was determined to see the matter through to the end. Jesus was talking and acting as if time was running out, so I did not think I would have long to wait. But I had a deeper reason for staying: I wanted to be with Jesus as long as possible. I didn't believe what he believed, but I had become bound to him. I cared deeply about this extraordinary—and extraordinarily deluded—man. As we continued up the winding road through deep ravines up toward Jerusalem, Jesus glanced back and saw me last in line. He nodded.

Pilgrims on their way to the Passover Festival gradually filled the road, jamming it and slowing down our progress. When some people in one of the caravans recognized Jesus, they spread the news amongst the travelers that Jesus was on his way to Jerusalem for the Passover. Soon people were running up to us and asking in excitement, "Is Jesus going to announce he's the king of Israel?" None of us knew what Jesus was planning, and our silence simply added fuel to the rumors. By midday, when we stopped at an oasis to rest, eagerness among the pilgrims had escalated to a fever pitch. Songs of Zion broke out spontaneously, sung at the top of everyone's lungs. After a short meal, we continued the ascent toward Jerusalem.

In the middle of the afternoon, weary from the steady climb and hot sun, we crested a hill and saw the walls of Jerusalem in the distance. Shouting erupted from the caravans, and then the singing resumed, even louder than before. As we passed through villages and people heard that Jesus was among the pilgrims, mothers ran up to us with their children, begging for Jesus to bless them. The Twelve pushed them away, tired of the constant attention. But Jesus, soaking up the energy and enthusiasm, reprimanded them.

"Let them come! God's empire belongs to them! Unless you receive God's empire like a child, you'll never enter it."

When we approached the villages of Bethphage and Bethany near the Mount of Olives, Jesus sent two of his disciples into the villages to look for a young donkey. "Tell the owner I need it and will return it soon."

In the eleven months since I had begun traveling with Jesus, he had gone everywhere on foot. But now he suddenly required a donkey? I immediately realized he intended to enact a symbol. A thousand years ago, Solomon had ridden into Jerusalem on a mule to be anointed king; now Jesus would repeat that ancient pattern. The prophet Zechariah had prophesied that a king would enter Jerusalem on the foal of a donkey, bringing an end to all war and establishing a worldwide empire of peace. Jesus meant to fulfill that dream. This was the climactic moment: either disaster or a miracle lay ahead.

The disciples returned with a colt and threw their cloaks over its back. Jesus sat on it and then proceeded down the road toward the gates of Jerusalem. As the pilgrims caught on to the symbolism of what Jesus was doing, they went wild. In a frenzy they cut leafy branches off the trees and threw them on the road in front of Jesus, or they took off their cloaks and spread them out to create a royal carpet. As Jesus rode forward, everyone began shouting a mix of blessings:

"Hosanna in the highest heaven! Blessed is he who comes in the name of the Lord! Blessed is the coming empire of David!"

The royal procession continued down the Mount of Olives, across the Kidron Valley, and up the steep hill to the Water Gate of Jerusalem. Jesus passed through the gate and up the avenue, passing through the Valley Gate and on toward the Temple Mount. Arriving there, he dismounted the colt and climbed the broad stairway to the Huldah Gates, through the tunnel and up into the temple courtyard, all the while surrounded by cheering crowds.

For several minutes Jesus stood in the midst of the massive plaza as pilgrims from all over Galilee, Perea, and Judea, as well as people from Jerusalem, thronged around him chanting: "God's empire! God's empire! God's empire!" As they shouted, Jesus looked around, watching the activities of the buyers, sellers, and money changers in the courtyard. I could see the wheels turning in his head as he was planning something. But it was late. The sun was going down, and this was not the best time to take action. So, blessing the crowd and exhorting them to return in the morning, Jesus left the temple courtyard. We retreated to Bethany, returned the colt, and then had dinner at the home of Martha and Mary.

The next morning, he made his way again to Jerusalem and the temple. He took his time, gathering pilgrims along the way. He wanted the crowds, camped all over the Mount of Olives, to see him and join him. By the time we reached the temple courtyard, the crowd was just as large as the day before, though not as frenzied. Instead, the mood was tense.

Jesus strode over to a table where men were changing Roman coins for the imageless "temple coins" that could be used to pay the temple tax. Grabbing the corner of the table, he heaved with all his might and flipped it over. Coins went flying everywhere. He then bounded over to a booth where merchants were selling sacrificial doves. He shouted at them to get out of the way and then kicked over their stools. He was acting like a madman, and everyone scattered out of his way. Then he shouted: "This is a house of prayer, but you have made it a hideout for robbers! God will destroy this temple and raise up a new one!"

Cheers erupted from the crowd. Now they understood what Jesus was doing: symbolically halting the operations of the temple and announcing its doom, much as the prophet Jeremiah had done six hundred years ago. Our continued indifference to the plight of the poor and our hypocritical religious rituals were coming to an end. God's judgment was at hand.

Jesus continued his fiery speech: "Judgment is coming on you scribes! You like to walk around in long robes and be greeted with respect in the marketplaces and get the best seats in the synagogue and the places of honor at dinners. Meanwhile you eat up the property of widows and cover it up with prayers.

"Judgment is coming on you Sadducees! You say you are faithful to Moses but you're locking people out of God's empire. You're not even trying to enter; instead, you're blocking those who want to come in.

"Judgment is coming on you Pharisees! You make sure to give a tithe of your garden spices—mint, dill, cumin—while neglecting justice and mercy. With your traditions you strain out a gnat while swallowing a camel.

"Judgment is coming on you priests! You ritually clean the outside of the cup, but inside it is full of greed. First clean the inside of the cup so the outside will be clean as well! You are like unmarked graves—people walk over them without knowing it."

By now, a number of temple police had shown up, but the crowd pushed them back and would not let them through to arrest Jesus. Since he was no longer knocking over tables and chairs, the police decided to back down and let him speak—as prophets have been doing in the temple for hundreds of years.

Some of the chief priests marched into the plaza, demanding to approach Jesus. Jesus signaled to the crowd to let them through.

"By what authority are you disrupting the functioning of the temple and pronouncing judgment?" one of them shouted.

Jesus shouted back: "I'll tell you if you can tell me by what authority John baptized people and pronounced judgment!"

The priests were stuck. John was revered by the people (if not by the scribes and priests). He was considered a genuine prophet acting by God's authority. That was not something the priests would ever admit, but neither could they afford to denounce him.

One of the priests said, "We don't know."

Jesus shrugged. "Then there's no point in my telling you where my authority comes from."

The crowd guffawed. The priests left, but it was clear they weren't giving up. Jesus continued preaching in the plaza for the rest of the day, hour after hour, announcing the coming of God's empire and the need to radically change our lives. When evening approached, he and his entourage once again headed for Bethany.

That night we stayed at the home of a former leper named Simon. While we reclined for supper, a woman came into the dining room with an alabaster jar of imported perfume. She broke off the head of the jar and poured the entire contents over Jesus's head. The fragrance filled the entire house, overpowering us. I was indignant at the enormous waste. I wasn't the only one. Matthew, one of the Twelve who was reclining near me, muttered, "We could have sold that perfume for a year's wages and fed every poor person in this village for a month." I glanced over at Judas. Frowning, he seemed to be doing the same mental calculation. When you live by begging, you learn to hate waste.

"Leave her alone," Jesus responded softly. "Don't object when someone acts with great generosity. She has served me. She has prepared my body ahead of time for burial."

There it was again: talk of death. Did he believe God's empire was about to triumph, or that he was about to die? It didn't make sense.

The next two days we were back in the temple courtyard, under Solomon's Portico. I noticed that the temple guard was out in full force, standing by all the vendors, making sure there would be no repeat of Jesus's symbolic protest. The crowd around Jesus was increasingly enthusiastic as he took on the religious elites and bested them. Each day the crowd was larger than the day before as the drama moved to its climax. The moment of truth was upon us: either Jesus would become the Messiah during this Passover Festival, leading God's empire to victory, or he would go down in defeat. Distraught, I knew which way it had to go.

On the third day that he was preaching, I recognized a scribe making his way through the crowd. He had worked for Herod's government and now worked for the temple. I hoped he would not see me—it would be difficult to explain why I was with Jesus—so I ducked behind Andrew. The silver-haired scribe signaled he wanted to ask a question. Jesus paused.

"Teacher, we know you're a straight talker. You tell it like it is whether it's popular or not. You're uncompromising when it comes to God's truth. So tell us: is it consistent with God's law to pay taxes to the Roman emperor? Should we pay his tax or not?"

My heart sank. This question was clearly designed to get Jesus arrested, not by the temple police, but by the Romans themselves. Their garrison overlooked the temple courtyard, and I'm sure they had paid informants everywhere. If Jesus said it was lawful to pay taxes to Caesar Tiberius, he would be morally emasculated, undermining his credibility with his supporters. But if he said it was not lawful to pay taxes to Rome, he would be on an almost certain path to execution.

Jesus shook his head in disappointment. "Why are you stooping so low with a trap question?"

The scribe did not respond but waited patiently for an answer. The crowd held its breath.

"Do you have a denarius?" asked Jesus.

The scribe pulled a pouch from under his shirt and fished out a little silver coin.

"Let me see it."

The scribe handed it over.

"Whose head is on this coin?" asked Jesus as he held out the silver disk between his fingers.

"Caesar's," answered the scribe.

"And whose name circles the image?"

The scribe bent forward to make sure and then answered, "Caesar Tiberius."

"If it has his image and his name on it, then it must belong to him. Give it back to him."

Jesus flicked the coin dismissively in the air; the scribe lunged to catch it.

"But give to God," shouted Jesus, "what belongs to God!"

True to form, Jesus managed to be vague and revolutionary at the same time. He could not be accused of forbidding the payment of Rome's taxes, but he was rejecting Rome's currency and the empire it supported. It was the cleverest answer I ever heard him give, but it also stung me the deepest. I could not help but think of the denarii waiting in my bank account because of what I was doing to Jesus.

XXII

THE NEXT MORNING JESUS did not go to the temple or into Jerusalem. Instead, he sent Andrew and Thaddaeus into the city to secretly arrange for the Passover dinner that evening for himself and the inner circle of the Twelve. It was the one night of the festival when he felt obligated to eat dinner in Jerusalem rather than in the safety of Bethany. Andrew and Thaddaeus returned a few hours later and told him everything was prepared. As the sun was setting, all of us left Bethany and walked toward Jerusalem. As we came down the slope of the Mount of Olives, Jesus turned aside at a place called Oil Press. He asked me and the other disciples who were not part of the Twelve to pitch camp there. That's where we would all be sleeping that night. Then he and the Twelve walked on into Jerusalem.

While Jesus and the Twelve celebrated Passover dinner in Jerusalem, the rest of us cooked some pieces of lamb and unleavened bread over an open fire and had our own Passover observance. The Mount of Olives was covered with pilgrims camping; little fires glowed all over the slope as we all shared wine and recalled the time when God rescued our ancestors from slavery and led them into freedom.

Later that night, just as we were lying down on our cloaks to sleep, Jesus and the Twelve stumbled through the darkness into our campsite. In the glow of the fire I could see from their faces they were upset and agitated. I whispered to Philip, asking what was wrong. He didn't want to talk about it. I looked for Judas to ask him, but I couldn't find him. Jesus then took his bodyguards—Rock and the Sons of Thunder—and walked off into the darkness. I laid down my head and closed my eyes, but just as I was drifting into sleep I heard Jesus crying out in the darkness: "Abba! Abba! Everything is possible for you—take away this cup!"

I had never heard Jesus so anguished. I continued to hear him moaning and jagged fragments of his pleading. It unnerved me.

I don't know how much time passed—I may or may not have fallen asleep—but the next thing I knew there was a commotion nearby: the sound of tramping feet, muffled voices, and then the flickering of a couple of torches. I propped myself up on my elbows and saw Judas walking toward me, holding a torch, followed by several temple police carrying clubs and swords. Judas looked this way and that at the sleeping figures on the ground. Then I heard Jesus's voice out of the darkness say, "Here I am."

Judas took a few steps forward until his torch lit up Jesus who was standing by himself. "Teacher," said Judas softly, and then kissed Jesus on the cheek.

I had a sudden, sick realization that I was not the only spy among Jesus's disciples. City Man had been working for the Jerusalem government.

Immediately the police stepped forward, knocked Jesus to the ground, and began tying his arms behind his back. One of the pilgrims, who had been camping nearby, attacked the police, swinging a dagger, slicing off someone's ear, but he was quickly disarmed.

Believing we were all about to be arrested, we jumped up and ran off in random directions, up and down the slopes of the Mount of Olives, in between the many campfires and tents, through the olive trees, and into the night. Aimlessly darting here and there in confusing directions, I soon doubled over, out of breath. My panic subsided when I realized no one was chasing me. Now where should I go? I found a depression under an olive tree, pulled my cloak around me, and huddled against the earth as the darkness became increasingly cold and windy. My teeth chattered through the rest of the night, as much from terror as from the stabbing wind.

When the rays of the sun came creeping down the face of the temple in the distance, I yearned to never move again, to just crumple into dust. But I needed to know what happened to Jesus. Staggering up, I brushed off my cloak and walked toward the gates of Jerusalem. The city quickly came to life and the streets were soon choked with vendors and pilgrims. I headed to the house of the high priest, Caiaphas, who lived in a lavish palace on a ridge overlooking the city and the western side of the Temple Mount. In the outer courtyard, slaves bustled with their work. I asked one of them whether he knew what happened to the man from Nazareth. He looked at me rudely, as if I was a terrorist, and told me that the Nazarene had gotten a good beating and then been handed over to the Roman prefect.

I walked to the palace of Pontius Pilate. Earlier in the week, he had ridden into Jerusalem with an armed guard to oversee security during the volatile Passover Festival. Closer to the heart of the city, the crowds were thick by his gates. I mingled among the beggars, asking if they had heard or seen anything about Jesus's arrest. Most wouldn't speak to me without receiving money, which I didn't have. The few who would talk to me were drunk or crazy. Feeling famished and tired, my dignity gone, my life empty, I slumped to the ground among the beggars and began to beg.

About an hour later, just as a pilgrim shared a piece of bread with me, I saw activity behind the gates. Some soldiers emerged from one of the buildings, leading a group of three prisoners in loin cloths and leg irons. The third prisoner, in particular, was a bloody mess. Half the skin on his back had been ripped off, probably by the thirty-nine lashes of a Roman whip studded with metal and bone. The man staggered, his face so swollen I didn't recognize him. But when I saw his feet, those feet alongside which I had walked countless miles, I knew who it was. Each of the three criminals held a long log across his shoulder, a beam upon which he would be nailed and hung. I dropped my piece of bread on the ground.

The soldiers unlocked the iron gate, swung it open, and ordered the prisoners into the street—five soldiers in front and five behind. The thick crowd parted, leery of the soldiers, and looked away from the prisoners as if pretending this wasn't happening. Slowly the troop of soldiers and condemned men shuffled their way down the street. The third prisoner fell repeatedly, buckling under the weight of his beam. After yet another fall, no number of kicks and curses enabled the broken man to pick up his beam. Furious, the centurion in charge grabbed a pilgrim on the edge of the crowd and ordered him to carry the criminal's beam. Terrified, the pilgrim obeyed. The troop moved on, the third prisoner staggering back and forth.

They made their way through the Gennath Gate past the Tower Pool and then turned aside at a rise called Skull Hill where crucifixions take place. On an outcrop of rock stood several posts. The soldiers ordered the condemned men to lie down on their backs, then grabbed their hands and stretched out their arms on the beams they had carried while another soldier hammered a nail through each wrist into the beam. The first two condemned men screamed; the third one, almost unconscious, let out a groan. The soldiers stripped off each prisoner's loincloth and then hoisted each end of the beam into the air and onto the top of a post, fitting it into a slot cut in the beam. Hanging from their wrists, the prisoners all let out shrieks. The soldiers grabbed their ankles and quickly nailed them to the sides of the posts.

Naked, the three criminals hung there, gasping for air. Pushing themselves up on their pinned ankles, they desperately sucked some air into their lungs to stay alive. It was the most torturous, humiliating, and slow execution the Romans could devise, terrorizing the population into never opposing the Roman empire.

A soldier nailed a placard above the head of each criminal, naming his crime. Two read: "Robber." One read: "King of the Jews."

I heard women wailing. Turning, I saw on the far side of the road Mary of Magdala huddling with several of the other women from Galilee. They had been staying at the home of Martha in Bethany. Somehow they must have heard about Jesus's arrest and come this morning into Jerusalem to find Jesus.

My brain didn't want to accept what was happening. I kept thinking this was not real, that I would soon wake from this nightmare. Instead, the nightmare was reality. Just when I thought I could not be more horrified, some of the priests came down the road, approached the execution grounds, and laughed.

"He said he'd destroy the temple, but look who's been destroyed! Hey, Messiah, come down from your cross and we'll believe in you!"

Even the two robbers began taunting him. One of them sputtered between quick breaths, "Save us, you fraud!"

For half the day I stood by the side of the road as pilgrims streamed in and out of the city, most averting their eyes from the gruesome spectacle. The flogged and beaten man groaned as he repeatedly tried to push himself up enough to breathe, but he kept sliding down when he lost strength. Once he gasped that he was thirsty, and someone grabbed a sponge, soaked it in wine, stuck it on a stick, and lifted it to his lips. Then he cried out:

"My God! Abba! My God! Why have you abandoned me!"

His words, echoing one of the Psalms, tore apart my heart. This man, who had put the deepest trust in God, was now crushed with despair. Whatever little faith I may have had in him shriveled into lifelessness.

About three o'clock he groaned loudly; then his strength gave out, and he sagged on the cross. Soon the heaving of his chest stopped, tremors in his shoulders and legs ceased, and his body became as still as the post on which he was nailed. I sat down and held my head in my hands. I knew then what I had long suspected but never allowed myself to admit—that life has no meaning or purpose, and the universe is blind and cruel. An appalling thought blotted out all sunlight: *There is no God worthy of worship. Government is God.*

Jesus's spell was broken.

An hour later a well-dressed man approached the centurion. He held out a parchment. The centurion read it and then gave him permission to remove the corpse. With the help of another man, they wrenched out the nails with some tools, lowered the bloody body, and carried it away. I followed them, as did the women across the street. The two men took the corpse to a nearby cemetery, placed it inside a tomb cut out of the rock, and rolled a millstone across the opening. I was about to say a prayer, but then wondered, what was the point?

The sun was about to set, marking the beginning of the Sabbath. It was too late to get to Bethany, and I did not want to sleep again on the Mount of Olives. I remembered a house in Jerusalem belonging to an Essene where we had frequently stayed when Jesus was in Jerusalem for the Feast of Booths. I thought it likely Jesus and the Twelve had celebrated their Passover dinner there last night. Might the householder give me lodging?

I made my way quickly through the streets and to the home of the Essene. He answered the door himself, and before I could even open my mouth he waved me up a flight of outer stairs to a door. He knocked, said his name, and I heard a bolt slide back from the other side. The door opened to an upper room, and there inside, to my astonishment, I saw the Twelve bunched up on the floor. All of them except Judas.

Distraught and traumatized, they had each gradually reconvened at the place of their final supper with Jesus. Although one of the women had come by and told them Jesus had been crucified, they didn't know he was already dead. I reported to them what I had witnessed. Their depression deepened.

A servant brought in a platter of bread and figs and a jug of wine, but nobody ate or drank anything. There were some hushed whispers discussing what they should do or where they should go, but no one had any answers. They all relied on Rock to decide the next step, but he wasn't saying anything.

I can't remember what happened the rest of that night or the next day. It's all a fog of emptiness, hopelessness, and pointlessness for me. The next night someone suggested we should leave for Galilee first thing on Sunday morning. That made sense to me. I certainly didn't want to stay in Jerusalem. It was time for me to leave this tragedy, go to Herod's palace in Tiberias, and give Theodorus my final report. I would tell him the crisis was over. Herod's government and Pilate's government had endured. The world was safe again for now. Unfortunately, the wrong side had won.

XXIII

ON SUNDAY MORNING, AS we were stuffing our travel bags with some extra food, we heard pounding on the bolted door. We immediately thought it was the police, but when Rock looked through the hole, he saw Mary of Magdala and two other women—Salome and Mary of Bethany—standing on the other side. When Rock opened the door, they hurried in, a look of horror on their faces.

"His tomb has been broken into!" blurted out Mary of Magdala. "His body has been stolen!"

The news shocked us all. As I pondered Mary's report, a sickening explanation came to my mind. As a famed healer, Jesus's corpse would be worth a lot of money. Every magician in Jerusalem would want to get their hands on Jesus's fingers, teeth, organs, and bones to turn them into amulets, or to grind them up into powders for potions.

Rock asked the women if they were sure they had gone to the right tomb. They insisted they had; they had gone to his tomb on Friday afternoon, following the men who had buried him. Rock turned to us and said he would check it out. He then left with the women so they could show him the way, and we bolted the door behind him.

Waves of despair swept over the room as we waited for Rock to return. Time dragged as a couple of hours went by. He should have been back in half that time. Just as we became convinced he had been nabbed by the police, a fist pounded on the door and we heard Rock's heavy voice.

John unbolted the door, swung it open, and Rock stepped in with the most confused look I've ever seen.

"Is his tomb empty?" asked one of the Twelve.

Rock nodded slowly.

"What did you see?"

Without looking at us, Rock responded, "His grave clothes."

We couldn't get any more information out of him. He just sat on the floor in puzzlement. I didn't know what was going on inside his head, but I'd had enough.

"I'm going home to Sepphoris," I announced.

No one responded. No one cared. I grabbed my bag, opened the door, and left.

As I walked toward the Damascus Gate, I wondered about that tomb. Was the women's report accurate? Had they indeed gone to the right tomb? I wanted to see it for myself. I changed direction and headed for the gate nearest to Skull Hill. Traffic through the streets was thick with pilgrims leaving town. I passed through the gate and turned right into the cemetery. Within a few paces I found the little cave tomb, and sure enough, the millstone was rolled back. I walked up to the black hole in the face of the rock and looked in. On the right was the shelf where his corpse had been laid. The corpse was gone.

I stood up to leave when Rock's report registered in my brain. I stooped down and looked again: the corpse was gone but the burial wrappings were lying on the shelf. Why had someone unwrapped the body? If you're going to steal a corpse, why take the time to unwrap it and then carry away a naked body? Maybe those two men who buried him just before Friday evening decided to move his body to another burial on Saturday evening, after the Sabbath was over. But even if they had, the question remained: why unwrap the body? No explanation came to my mind. It was another crazy puzzle to add to so many about Jesus. With Jesus, nothing was ever fully clear.

I stood up once again and walked away, and I didn't stop until I was very far from Jerusalem.

XXIV

I THOUGHT THAT WOULD be the end of the story.

A week later I arrived at Herod's palace in Tiberias. Running the gauntlet of security and bureaucracy, I made a final report directly to Theodorus, assuring him Jesus was dead and his followers dispersed and dispirited.

"A satisfactory result," he mumbled. As he sat in his chair, he looked down to read a scroll rolled out on his desk, dismissing me with silence.

"Sir," I added hesitantly, "what was decided about my pay?"

His red, watery eyes looked at me with impatience.

"Go see the pay master."

I bowed, thanked him, and left his room. I wound my way through the corridors of the palace to the office of the pay master, wondering the whole way whether I'd receive anything at all. It would be just like Herod's government to stiff me. So I was quite surprised when the pay master handed me a heavy sack. Checking a ledger, he said, "Six hundred denarii, minus three hundred that was sent to your wife in ten monthly installments of thirty each."

I was holding in my hand a small fortune. Thanks to nearly a year of living off the generosity of others, I had managed to save a sizeable amount of money. A feeling of glee filled me as I imagined all the things I would buy once I was home in Sepphoris: new robes and sandals, some jewelry for my wife and daughter, a new roof and stove for the house, a feast of tender lamb with plenty of good-quality wine, and—best of all—a sauna in the Roman bath-house. No more living like a filthy beggar! I would be respectable again.

When I returned home, the delightful reunion did not go as I expected. Perhaps my first words should not have been, "I'm home, woman."

My wife, on her knees digging in the garden, stopped to stare at me for a few seconds, and then resumed her digging.

Indignation seized me. "No greeting for your husband?"

She stopped digging again and looked at me coldly. "My husband has been gone for nearly a year. You abandoned me and our daughter."

"I did not abandon you!" I sputtered. "I was forced to do a job—a miserable job. I often had to sleep in barns and ditches and eat whatever scrap was thrown to me. What I was doing had to be kept secret. I couldn't tell you. And now I come home after all of my misery and all I receive is your hard heart!"

Even as I said the words, I knew they were not the whole truth. I could have sent her a message telling her I was safe. I could have told her I was on a government assignment and did not know when I would be home. The embarrassing fact was I was so emotionally engaged during those extraordinary months, I rarely thought about my wife.

"You received money each month, didn't you?" I added defensively. "And look, I have plenty more silver in this bag."

She said nothing and resumed digging.

A little later I saw my daughter. She acted as if she hardly remembered me, as if I was a traveling salesman who comes round once a year.

Fine, be that way. Over the next few days I bought a new robe, a pair of sandals, and some jewelry; I got the roof and stove repaired; I gave my wife extra money for the food allowance; and I spent one afternoon at the bathhouse. But all of it was joyless. It was just stuff.

As soon as possible I went back to work sorting records. I needn't have worried about someone else messing up my records, because I soon discovered that Herod's government never assigned anyone to fill in for me. What incompetent skinflints! I was immediately drowning in nearly a year's worth of unfinished work. After spending another few weeks in Sepphoris, I gave my sullen wife a quick goodbye and was on the road again collecting records throughout Galilee.

About a month later I arrived in Cana, where I heard the most bizarre rumor: the Twelve were in Jerusalem claiming Jesus had been raised from the dead. They were insisting that this proved Jesus was the Messiah of God's empire and should now be called "Lord," as if he was the Roman emperor exercising all the power and glory of the gods.

I shook my head in exasperation and sorrow. What kind of desperate delusion was this? Why couldn't the Twelve face reality? Unable to get the rumor out of my head, I determined to travel to Jerusalem to see for myself whether the Twelve were really making these pitiful claims. I left Cana as soon as was feasible and hurried toward Jerusalem. But as I walked the long roads, my anxiety rose with each passing day, filling me with traumatic memories and dread. By the time I passed through the gates of Jerusalem, every muscle in my body quivered as I stumbled in the gathering darkness of nightfall.

Heading toward the house of the Essene, where I had last seen the Twelve, I tried to calm myself with deep breaths. By the time I arrived at the house, darkness blanketed the city, but I saw a dim, flickering light coming through a second story window. Carefully ascending the outer stairway, I hesitated for several seconds before knocking softly on the door. A moment later a familiar face opened the latch: Philip. Smiling, he grabbed my arm, pulled me in, and embraced me. Behind him, reclining on a mat, eating a pomegranate from a plate, I saw Rock.

"Watcher, eat with us!" he bellowed.

In the gloom of the room I saw the Sons of Thunder, as well as several other men I didn't recognize, also reclining on mats. I picked a place on the floor next to Philip.

"You must have heard the good news!" shouted Rock again, even more boisterously.

"Well, I heard something," I said. "I'm surprised you fellows are still here in Jerusalem. I thought you were all going back to Galilee."

Rock smiled from ear to ear. "We did. We wanted to get as far from those temple police as we could! So I went back to the lake and started my fishing business again. But let me tell you what happened then."

He paused and looked knowingly at James and John before proceeding. "One night I was out on my boat fishing with my crew. James and John were on another boat with their crew. Anyway, neither boat was catching anything. We dragged those nets through half the lake all night long and never caught a minnow! Then, just as the sky was turning pink on the horizon, a guy on the shore shouts to me, 'Have you caught anything?' I was really annoyed and shouted back, 'No!' He then shouts, 'Cast your nets on the other side of the boat.' Now I was really steamed. I didn't need this idiot's advice on how to fish. But my crew suggested we give it a try—maybe the guy could see something from shore that we couldn't see. So we pull up the nets and cast them on the other side. And you know what happened?" Rock paused, his face full of excitement.

"No, what happened."

"The net filled with fish! I mean right away! And I don't mean some fish, I mean a whole school of fish so big that we couldn't even haul it into the boat! I had to shout to James and John to come over with their boat and help us haul in the net. Even with all of us working together, we couldn't get that net out of the water, it was so heavy with fish!"

"Yeah," I responded, still waiting for Rock to get to the point.

"Don't you see? It was Jesus!"

"What was Jesus?"

"The man on the shore!"

I paused. "What do you mean?"

Rock's eyes sparkled as he drew in his breath. "The first time Jesus ever spoke to me—almost a year and a half ago—I'm on my boat, a little ways from shore, casting a net into the lake. I hear this man shout to me, 'Follow me and I'll show you how to fish for people!' I turn around and see Jesus. I knew who he was because I had heard him preaching in town the day before. I couldn't believe that this great prophet wanted me to follow him! I dropped everything and joined him. That moment is burned into my memory. Well, a few weeks ago, when that stranger shouted for me to cast my net on the other side and it immediately filled with the largest catch of fish I've ever seen in my life, well I just knew it—it was Jesus. It had to be!"

I didn't know how to respond to his idiocy. I settled for a non-committal "I'm not understanding what you're saying."

"Don't you get it? Jesus's tomb was empty—and it was empty because God raised him from the dead!"

"So the man on the beach . . . was actually Jesus?"

"Yes! I jumped into the lake and swam ashore. There he was, sitting on some rocks, cooking a fish on a small fire. He greeted me. He knew my name. But he didn't look like Jesus. He looked like a different person."

"I'm sorry, now I'm really confused."

"It didn't look like him, but I knew it was him. I didn't have to ask him. I knew and he knew I knew. A little later, James and John brought the boats ashore. We all had breakfast with him, cooking some of our fish over his fire. We all knew, without saying a word, that we were with Jesus."

I glanced over at the Sons of Thunder, expecting them to surreptitiously roll their eyes at Rock's story, but instead they solemnly nodded to me.

"But why didn't Jesus look like Jesus?"

"Because Jesus isn't just Jesus anymore. He's been raised up to God in heaven! He's changed. He's the Messiah that God has prepared since the foundation of the world!"

My face must have betrayed my incredulity.

"Watcher, we're not the only ones who have seen him. The Twelve have seen him. Others have seen him. He's been seen in visions and seen face-to-face, seen in heaven and seen on earth. We who have seen him have been chosen to be his messengers—which is why we've all come back to Jerusalem."

I couldn't make sense of anything he was telling me. I thought he had lost his mind.

"The Twelve—all of you—have seen him?"

The brightness in his face and voice faded as he said, "All but Judas."

An image came into my mind of Judas kissing Jesus, identifying him in the darkness for the temple police. I shuddered as I asked softly, "What happened to Judas?"

"He's dead," answered Rock flatly.

"How?" I asked in surprise.

"I don't know, and I don't care. Maybe he was knifed by someone. Maybe he took his own life. All I heard is that somebody found his bloody corpse out in a field. Maybe it was guilt. Maybe it was revenge. Either way, it had to be connected to him getting paid to finger Jesus."

A red-hot dagger plunged into my heart. I jumped up and ran from the room, down the flight of stairs, and into the darkness of the streets. As I sought escape in the black maze of backstreets, tears burst from my eyes. At some point I fell in the offal and waste of an alley, blubbering uncontrollably. A long time passed before I felt a hand on my shoulder. I jolted, not knowing who was there.

"Watcher," whispered Rock. "Come back."

I had never known Rock, that big oaf, to be tender. He sounded like Jesus, which only increased my pain.

"I can't."

"Why not?"

Heaving with suppressed secrets, my brain stopped working and my emotions took over completely. I couldn't hold it in anymore. Furiously, I shouted, "Because I betrayed Jesus! And I got paid too!"

The calloused hand on my shoulder suddenly clenched and then pulled away.

I looked up but the alley was so black I couldn't see Rock. "Punch me, Rock! I was a spy! Paid by Herod! Punch me!"

He said nothing, but I could vaguely make out the outline of his massive form and hear his breath sucking in through his nostrils. I scrabbled on the ground and clutched a loose paving stone.

"Here! Here's a large stone! Strike me! Stone me!"

The hulk of his form did not move. He remained silent.

"Speak, you clod! Curse me! Damn me to hell! You know what I did with that money? I took a bath at the Roman bathhouse. And I bought jewelry! Wouldn't Jesus be proud!"

Rock said nothing. In the distance a cock crowed.

I thought we might remain in that filthy alley all night. We just sat there, silent except for the sound of our breathing. Then Rock finally spoke.

"I betrayed Jesus too."

Jesus's right-hand man and unshakable defender—betrayed Jesus? I was too shocked to say anything.

"I've never told anyone this," came a quiet voice in the gloom. "When Jesus was arrested, I followed the police. They took Jesus to the house of Caiaphas. It was a freezing night; there was a fire lit in the courtyard where the slaves were keeping themselves warm. I crept into the courtyard and warmed my hands at the fire. A girl kept staring at me. I tried to avoid her eyes. Finally she says, 'You're one of the followers of Jesus, aren't you?' I said I wasn't. I said I didn't even know what she was talking about. But she started telling the other slaves, 'This guy's one of the followers of that Nazarene.' Again I insisted she was wrong. But then this nasty-looking fellow says, 'Sure you are! I can tell by your accent that you're from Galilee!' I was so scared I swore by God and the lives of my children that I'd never even heard of Jesus—and that Jesus could go to hell."

As I caught my breath at this confession, I heard him begin to wail and saw his great shoulders heave. Incredulous, I thought to myself, *Rock turned into sand*. Instinctively I reached out my hand to touch him. He then clasped me and we sobbed together.

A soft rain began to fall, slowly soaking our heads and clothing, and then Rock whispered in my ear, "That man on the beach told me, 'Feed my sheep.' Who could have told me that but Jesus?"

For a moment, Rock's fantastic claims didn't seem quite so fanciful. Some strange bud had sprouted out of the hardest absurdity.

After a while, he gave me a pat on the back. "Watcher, you know who you are?"

Spy, *betrayer*, *bastard*—those were the words that came to my mind. Instead, I shook my head.

"You're a lost sheep, and the shepherd is looking for you."

XXV

I STAYED IN JERUSALEM for two weeks, and what I witnessed astonished me. No longer an itinerant movement, the Twelve had brought their families to Jerusalem and put down roots, establishing an ongoing community of Jesus's followers. To maintain the claim that they were spiritually reconstituting the nation of Israel, Judas's place among the Twelve was filled by another long-time disciple, Matthias. Every day Rock and John went to the temple, preaching that God had raised Jesus from the dead and challenging people to reform their lives, embrace Jesus as the Messiah, and join the Messiah's community by being baptized.

Joining the community entailed generously sharing with one another: property, wealth, food, and clothing. As a result, the Twelve were in the process of eliminating destitution among Jesus's followers, as well as among many others in Jerusalem. No one had too much, and everyone had enough. The entire group met frequently to eat together, pray, and learn from the Twelve how to live as Jesus had taught. While I was there, the community grew.

How could Peter and John be so brave? How could they preach about Jesus—executed for sedition—right under the noses of the Roman government and the temple authorities? They risked arrest or stoning every day, but they persisted. What Jesus had sowed in Galilee was blooming in Jerusalem. A feeling of awe rose within me: *Might this be God's government—or something like it, something that will lead us in a healing direction?*

One Sunday—the day of the week on which they said Jesus had been raised—we gathered for a dinner together. Mary of

Magdala reclined with us and was treated as an honored member of the community. Rock broke the bread and said it was Jesus's body. He passed a jug of wine and said it was Jesus's blood. By eating and drinking this meal we were binding ourselves to Jesus's life and love, and Rock said Jesus himself would be among us. As he spoke, out of the corner of my eye, I caught a glimpse of a ghost. I nearly screamed in fright when I saw Jesus.

But with a second look I realized I was mistaken. It wasn't Jesus, but someone who looked so similar he could have been his twin: his younger brother James. What was James doing here, I wondered. The last time I saw any of Jesus's family, they were trying to convince him to leave Capernaum and go back to Nazareth because they thought he was losing his mind.

After dinner, I approached James. "I remember you," he said to me. "You were the oddest one among a group of odd ones."

"And I remember you," I responded. "You were the sober, pious brother. I'm surprised you're here. I don't remember you or anyone in Nazareth wanting to follow Jesus."

"That was before he appeared to me," he said, his eyes glazed with memory. "Now the whole family is devoted to his cause. Our mother is living here as well."

The next morning I began my journey back to Sepphoris. Along the way, over the course of days, I had much to ponder. I thought about our ancestor Abraham laughing at God when God told him his barren and elderly wife, Sarah, would give birth to a son. I thought about how Abraham, years later, was willing to sacrifice that son back to God, trusting that even in the face of absurdity and death, nothing is impossible for God. I thought about how Moses, in the face of Pharaoh's chariots, told the Hebrews that God would fight for them and that they had only to be still. I thought about how the Babylonians destroyed Jerusalem and the temple and took the people away as prisoners, but the prophets declared that if they trusted in God and carried out God's justice, they would return to Jerusalem and rebuild the temple and the nation. And in time, as if in a dream, it happened.

As one of the psalms says, "The stone rejected by the builders has become the cornerstone of the house, and it is marvelous in our eyes." God keeps doing this—building something surprising out of what we have discarded as hopeless.

As I passed through a rocky field blooming with wildflowers, a gust of wind rustled the grasses. A feeling stirred within me, deeper than reason, and I suddenly knew that something was at work in this world I could not see. I thought: *Maybe the meek will inherit the earth after all.*

The following day, an hour or two past midday, my feet grew tired and the sun beat down on my sweating brow. Feeling the oppression of the heat, I recalled Jesus being stripped, nailed, and tortured to death on a cross. The terrifying images devoured me from the inside out. But as I endured the memory of that horror, I wondered if this is what it takes for God to save us from ourselves. Must God show us love, be that love, even if it means humiliation, suffering, and death?

I thought of Mary of Magdala and the other women who traveled with Jesus or who sat at his feet. I remembered how Jesus shocked us by including these women among his followers and defended them against our verbal abuses. I recalled their wailing at Skull Hill as Jesus slowly died, and their devotion which drove them to his tomb early in the morning after the Sabbath. With shame I realized the women had proved to be the most faithful disciples.

When I passed through Tiberias, I stopped at the palace, asked to see the manager of records, and told him I was quitting my job with Herod's government. He was shocked. Maybe he thought I'd become an insurrectionist. I didn't care. All I knew was that I didn't believe in Herod's government anymore and I wanted no part in its functioning.

I arrived at my home in Sepphoris as the sun was setting and found my wife grinding meal in the kitchen with a mortar and pestle. She glanced at me indifferently and continued her monotonous labor. I drew in my breath, stuttered a bit, and then spoke softly.

"Judith, I have been a fool. I was wrong to have left you for so long and not to have assured you in some way. I have not loved you as I ought. How may I honor you now?"

She stopped grinding but did not look at me. I stepped behind her, reached around her waist and placed my hands on her hands. She dropped the pestle and her body trembled.

"I'm sorry," I whispered.

Our daughter sauntered into the kitchen, carrying a small sack of spice. Twelve years old, I had not realized she was already a beauty. Her mouth dropped open when she saw my arms around her mother. She turned away in embarrassment and was about to scurry away.

"Keziah, come here," I said with a hush.

Letting go of my wife, I reached out my arms to my daughter. She approached cautiously. The tips of my fingers rested on her shoulders and then gently pulled her toward me.

"I have not been a good father, Keziah. You are growing into a fine woman and I have missed it entirely. Forgive me."

"I forgive you," she said almost inaudibly.

It was a child's forgiveness, too quickly given to mean more than humble deference, but it might be a start.

I turned back to Judith. "If you are willing, let me tell you all that has happened."

Lighting a lamp, I settled on a mat, and Judith and Keziah sat down as well. I spoke with them late into the night, recalling everything: the wonders, the hardships, the questions, my complicity in the government's surveillance, and the fatal silencing of Jesus. And then I told them about the unexpected community sprouting in Jerusalem.

"What do you think of this story?" I asked.

Judith was quiet for a long time, the sawing of locusts filling the silence.

"It is a strange story. It frightens me."

"Why does it frighten you?"

"I am frightened by what it may have done to you."

Instantly I lowered my eyes, filled with dread by what I needed to reveal next.

"I quit my job with the government."

Judith's eyes flared as her mouth dropped open. "How will we live?" she gasped, shaking her head in astonished fear.

"By every word that comes from the mouth of God," I answered, remembering something Jesus had once said.

"No!" she cried and buried her face in her palms as she sobbed.

How foolish my words must have sounded to her. I felt embarrassed. But I meant what I said, or wanted to.

"Judith," I said softly, waiting for a pause in her moans, "I'm sorry. It was a decision I should not have made without your knowledge. But I could teach the law. Find students to train as scribes. I see the law now as if it were new. It may be a pauper's life, but it will be without shame."

The following days were a mixture of arguments and tears for both of us. Judith was right to be frightened. There is no easy or clear path ahead.

What do I believe? I'm not sure, but to truly live I must commit myself, and I know now I must commit myself to something better and greater than Herod's government and better and greater than myself. I cannot be a Watcher any longer.